860

P9-DML-706

Running Wild

Thomas J. Dygard

Running Wild

MORROW JUNIOR BOOKS
New York

In loving memory of
Edward and Louise Carmack

2   3   4   5   6   7   8   9   10

Library of Congress Cataloging-in-Publication Data
Dygard, Thomas J.
Running wild / Thomas J. Dygard
p. cm.
Summary: When Coach Wilson and Officer Stowell encourage
him to join the high school football team, Pete no longer believes that
"nobody does anything for nothing."
ISBN 0-688-14853-0
[1. Football—Fiction.   2. Friendship—Fiction.   3. High Schools—Fiction.
4. Schools—Fiction.]   I. Title.   PZ7.D9893Rw 1996   [Fic]—dc20
96-10182   CIP   AC

Chapter One

When the policeman brought Pete Holman out of the back room of the station house, Pete was surprised to see Coach Wilson standing on the other side of the counter.

Except for an officer seated at a desk, reading a magazine, the coach, Pete, and the officer escorting him were the only ones in the room at this hour on a Saturday night.

Pete knew Coach Wilson, of course, same as every other student at Cartwright High. He knew his background, too—a star quarterback at Cartwright High, who went away to college and then came back to his old high school in the Chicago suburbs to teach biology and coach the football team. How could anybody at Cartwright High help knowing all about him? Photos of Jack Wilson in action in his playing days were plastered all over the walls in the lobby of the gym, along with pictures of other football players from the past.

1

But Pete had never exchanged a word with Coach Wilson.

Well, almost never. There was the time that Pete punched out Alan Hollis because he had laughed and poked fun when Mrs. Snow read part of Pete's report on T. S. Eliot out loud. She had suggested Pete had copied it straight out of an encyclopedia. It didn't help that Mrs. Snow was right. Others in the class had laughed, too, but it was Alan who'd piped up with, "Pete Holman, the great scholar," which made everybody laugh even more.

So Pete had waited for Alan in the hallway after class and settled the score the way he usually did—with his fists. He had jumped him, backed Alan up against the wall, and punched him in the face. As luck would have it, Coach Wilson was coming out of his biology classroom and saw what happened. He ran up, grabbed Pete, and took him to the assistant principal's office. Probably he never even got Pete's name.

Besides, that was months ago, back last spring.

Yet here was Coach Wilson, standing on the other side of the counter in the police station.

The police officer said, "You know Coach Wilson." It was a statement, not a question.

Pete said, "Sure," but he didn't feel sure of much of anything right now—what was going on here?

He was the only one of the three who'd been

caught when they dived out of Bucky Cochran's car. The cop car had come out of nowhere after Bucky, skidding around a corner, sideswiped a parked car. Bucky and Jimbo Dunton got away in the dark. Bucky was pretty dumb to run. They were sure to catch up with him when they checked his license plates. But maybe Bucky had quit thinking straight when the siren and the flashing red light came on. Bucky sometimes wasn't very good at thinking straight, even in the best of circumstances. Whatever, Bucky jumped out with the other two and ran, and he and Jimbo got away. Bucky was sure to be caught in the end, but it looked like Jimbo was free.

Pete hadn't been so lucky. While Bucky and Jimbo piled out of the left side of the car and vanished in a yard full of shrubs, Pete jumped out of the front seat on the passenger side and found himself almost in the arms of an approaching cop. Pete tried to fake him out—a lowered shoulder, a little step to the right, and then a whirl and a run to the left. But the cop caught his arm. Pete gave a tug and then gave up. He didn't want to get into a wrestling match with a policeman. Besides, he figured, he wasn't the driver, so what was the problem? But the cop loaded him into the car with the lights flashing and drove him to the police station.

Sure, the three of them had had a few beers, and the bottles were in the car for the cop to see. But nobody was really drunk. And there was no law against driving around on a Saturday night. The cops had no real reason to hold him. But they had kept Pete in a back room for almost an hour. They hadn't questioned him about who the other boys were, or where they had gotten their beer, or anything. They just took his name, address, and telephone number and sat him down.

And now here was Coach Wilson. This was weird, all of it. Really weird.

Coach Wilson said, "Hi, Pete."

Pete just nodded.

The police officer spoke to Coach Wilson. "Like I told you, Jack, there was no answer at his home."

Pete gave out a snort. Of course there was no answer at his home. His mother worked nights as a nursing supervisor at Cartwright Memorial Hospital—something Pete had neglected to tell the police—and there was no one else to answer the telephone. No father, no brothers, no sisters. Pete's father, a petroleum engineer, had died in a plane crash while on assignment in Venezuela two years ago, shortly after moving the family to the Chicago area. Pete and his mother lived alone. Pete had expected the cop to come back and ask where his parents could be reached, but he never had.

Coach Wilson turned to Pete. "Bill—Officer

Stowell—called me when he couldn't reach anyone at your home."

"Why?"

Coach Wilson smiled for the first time. "He thought you might rather have someone sign you out and take you home than sit around here until he got hold of someone at your house."

Pete frowned. "Okay," he said. "But why you?"

"I'm getting to that. I'll sign you out of here.... But there are two conditions."

Alarm bells went off in Pete's brain. He'd heard that kind of talk before. All his life people had been trying to lay down some kind of rules with him— teachers, his parents, sometimes even his fellow students, and now a football coach, of all people. "Conditions? What conditions?"

Coach Wilson didn't answer the question. Instead, he asked, "Do you want me to sign you out of here?"

"Sure, sure," Pete said. Then he put on a scowl and said, "I just asked what conditions. Don't I have a right to know?"

Coach Wilson stared at Pete in silence.

Pete returned the coach's gaze for a moment and then looked away. He was almost sorry he had snapped at him. He certainly did not want to stay at the police station until his mother got home. She would ask all sorts of questions and probably give him a lecture. Besides, he didn't want to be here when the cops finally tracked down Bucky and brought him in with his old man. Mr. Cochran was always angry and shouting about something.

Coach Wilson glanced across at Officer Stowell and said, "Bill…"

"Why don't you go ahead, Jack, and we'll see."

Pete looked from one to the other and frowned. What was going on here?

Coach Wilson gave a little nod and turned to Pete. "The first condition is that I take you home and, even if nobody is there, you stay. It's close to twelve o'clock. You've got no business out running around."

Pete shrugged. "Okay. No problem." After the accident, he and the guys were through for the night anyway. Besides, he didn't even know where Bucky and Jimbo had scattered to by now.

Coach Wilson took a breath, raised his eyebrows, and went back to staring at Pete.

Pete shifted his weight from one foot to the other and waited. What was next?

"The other condition is that you turn out on Monday afternoon for football practice."

Pete blinked and his mouth opened slightly without any sound coming out. Having a bucket of cold water dumped on him from behind would have been less of a shock. He tried to grin. A grin was always his best defense, his best delaying tactic, when he didn't know what to say or do. A grin showed that Pete Holman hadn't been caught by surprise. Pete Holman was in control. But this time the grin wouldn't come.

Nobody said anything. Coach Wilson and Officer Stowell just stood there, watching him.

Finally, Pete found his voice. "Football? Me?"

In his mind, Pete could see Bucky's face, and Jimbo's. He could hear what they would have to say about Pete Holman's going out for football. Jimbo's first words would be "sold out," and those would not be his last words, nor his nastiest. Bucky would look confused and express amazement, and then he'd quickly join Jimbo in condemning Pete. Pete knew the routine.

Coach Wilson said, "Officer Stowell was a pretty good fullback in his day at Cartwright High, and he thinks you could carry the ball." He paused. "You look pretty strong to me, and"—he paused again and let a small smile cross his face—"Bill says you looked like you were pretty quick when you tried to fake him out. The Bulldogs can always use someone strong and quick."

Pete now gave the coach a sharp look. He'd heard that kind of talk before, like he owed Cartwright High something. A couple of years ago, not long after Pete had first showed up at the high school, a gym teacher had fed him a line about being fast enough to be a big help to the track team. Pete didn't buy it. He and his friends weren't into sweating for good ol' Cartwright High.

"Nah!" Pete said, almost on reflex. But then he thought about sitting in the police station another hour or so, and then having to go through yet another round with his mother. He said, "But I've never—"

"You can learn." It was Officer Stowell.

Pete saw Bucky's and Jimbo's faces again and heard their voices. He shook his head. "No way, man. No way at all."

Coach Wilson looked at Officer Stowell and shrugged his shoulders. Then the two of them looked at Pete.

Pete stood there for what seemed like hours. He took a deep breath. "Well, maybe," he said finally. "Maybe I'll give it a try."

"No maybes," Coach Wilson said firmly.

Pete nodded slowly. "Okay."

He figured he could decide later whether to keep the promise.

Chapter Two

Pete's mother woke him shortly after nine the next morning. "Phone," she said. "It's Bucky Cochran." His mother was still in her robe. Pete had heard her come in shortly after he had turned out his light and gotten into bed. Bucky's call had probably awakened her. She looked drowsy.

"Thanks," Pete said, and pulled himself into a sitting position on the side of the bed. He rubbed his eyes.

Then he stood up, stretched, and walked out into the hall and down to the living room. He picked up the phone from the small desk. "Hey!" he said.

"Did you get caught?"

The events of the evening before flashed through Pete's mind. "Yeah," he said.

"Anything happen?"

"They let me go after a while."

"That's all?"

Pete frowned. He didn't need to tell Bucky right away about his agreement to join the football team.

He wasn't even sure himself right now what he was going to do about it. Finally, he said in an exaggerated singsong voice, "I had to promise to be a good boy."

Bucky laughed, then said, "You're lucky."

"Did they trace the car and haul you in?"

"Worse than that. They came to the house. They woke up my folks and told them that the car was smashed up and they'd impounded it."

"Bummer."

"You bet. My folks screamed at me most of the night, and now I'm grounded. Indefinitely. And my ol' man says I've got to get a job or something to pay for the damage."

"That's bad. Real bad."

"You sound funny."

"I just woke up. That's all."

When Jimbo called shortly before noon, he was gloating. "I thought Bucky was pretty stupid to run," he said. "But, then, Bucky's pretty stupid most of the time, anyway." After a pause to let that one sink in, he asked, "How did you let yourself get caught?"

Pete held the phone for a moment without speaking, picturing Jimbo's leer of triumph. Jimbo had not been caught. He was calling Bucky stupid for running. And even though he wasn't calling Pete stupid for getting caught, he was coming close. Finally, Pete said only, "I think I ran the wrong way."

◆ ◆ ◆ ◆ ◆

In the hall between second and third periods on Monday morning, Pete stood outside the classroom door, waiting until the last minute before going in. Bucky appeared in front of him and said, "I've got to have a smoke. Let's go. We don't need this study hall anyway."

Pete shrugged and walked with him down the hall.

With a glance back to see if they were being watched, they walked out the front door and around the side of the building to the door leading down into the boiler room. It was the safest place to go for a cigarette while cutting a class. Nobody could see the area from inside the school building. The only threat was Mr. Hodges, the custodian, and chances were slim that he would come out the door in the middle of the morning.

They both lit up, and, after exhaling, Pete said, "I've got to tell you something before you find out from someone else."

"Oh?"

Pete grinned. "I'm going out for football."

Bucky's eyes widened, and he stared at Pete without speaking. Then he said, "You're *what*?"

Pete kept grinning and said nothing, enjoying the shock and confusion on Bucky's face. He also liked the idea of Bucky's knowing ahead of Jimbo—

a little payback for Jimbo's bragging about getting away on Saturday night.

"You're kidding," Bucky said. "Not you—football!"

Pete told Bucky about Coach Wilson's signing him out of the police station—and the conditions the coach had put on his action.

"But you're not going to do it," Bucky said.

"I've been thinking about it," Pete said.

"You mean you're really going to do it?"

"I promised," Pete said with a grin.

Bucky stared again in disbelief.

"But," Pete continued, "I didn't promise for how long."

Bucky thought a moment and then laughed. "You mean, like, you'll go out for football—for maybe thirty minutes."

"That might be about right," Pete said.

When Bucky blurted out the news to Jimbo at lunch, Jimbo gave Pete a quick glance, then turned back to Bucky and listened with a deepening frown. He did not enjoy being behind Bucky in hearing the news. And he always disapproved of the others taking any action that hadn't been cleared in advance with him.

When Bucky finished talking, Jimbo turned to Pete and said, "So ol' Petey wants to be a football star."

"Nah," Bucky said, leaning forward. "Didn't you hear what I said?"

Jimbo looked back at him. "Oh, ol' Petey wants to go out for football, all right. He wouldn't be doing it if he didn't want to, now would he? Ol' Petey doesn't have to do anything he doesn't want to. Isn't that right?"

Pete shifted uneasily in his seat. As always, Jimbo's goading remarks were hard to answer. If he said anything about needing to keep a promise, Jimbo was sure to shift his ridicule into high gear. Pete finally said, "I haven't really decided yet what I'm going to do."

"If you don't want to do it," Jimbo snapped, "just don't do it."

"It's not that easy."

"Sure it is. What are they going to do? Is that policeman going to come and arrest you for not going out for football? Is the coach going to hold you down while somebody forces shoulder pads on you?"

Pete didn't answer Jimbo's questions.

By the first class after lunch the attendance chart had caught up with Pete, and he was summoned to the administrative office.

Bucky was coming out as Pete went in. He gave Pete a lopsided grin, and Pete shrugged in return.

Pete walked in and stood in front of the assistant principal's desk. He knew the drill.

"You were marked absent in your third-period study hall," said Mr. Owen, a slightly built young man with a serious face. "Is there an explanation?"

Pete shrugged. "No, I guess not."

Mr. Owen watched him a moment. "The school year is just beginning. I was hoping you would be turning over a new leaf."

Pete grinned and waited. He had been in Mr. Owen's office so many times last year—for socking Alan Hollis, for smoking on the school grounds and in the boys' restroom, and for cutting classes—that he could almost mouth along with the assistant principal's next words.

"I'm assigning you to one day of early morning study hall, an hour before the first bell. You know the rule. If you miss it, or if you're late, you'll be assigned to two days of early morning study hall."

Pete nodded. Yes, he knew the rule.

Mr. Owen paused, then said, "I'm sorry to see you getting off on the wrong foot at the start of the new school year."

Pete shrugged and started to turn and leave.

But Mr. Owen wasn't finished. "You're a senior. You have this one last year to make a good record for yourself at Cartwright High. If you don't accept this opportunity, I'm afraid you will look back someday with regrets."

Pete frowned and said nothing.

Mr. Owen nodded his dismissal, and Pete walked out, to be picked up by the student clerk escorting him back to his class.

Without thinking, Pete said, "I know the way," same as he'd said every time he was summoned the previous year. He enjoyed watching the student clerk fumble for a reply.

This time, though, the student clerk didn't answer, and Pete walked along behind him, the frown coming back to his face.

When the bell rang, ending the last class, Pete sauntered out into the hall and looked around. At the end of the day he usually dumped off unneeded books in Bucky's locker, which was just outside the classroom. That way, he could be on his way quicker. He, Bucky, and Jimbo had one another's locker combinations. The arrangement was handy for dumping books, and sometimes for finding a cigarette. Pete carried his books across to Bucky's locker, opened it, and dropped the books in the bottom. There was no need to take them home. Anything that needed doing could be done in the boredom of the early morning study hall.

Before closing the door, Pete looked down the hallway. Seeing Bucky approaching, he waited with the door open.

"Are you really going to do it?" Bucky asked.

Pete had been asking himself the same question all afternoon. Jimbo was correct. He didn't have to go out for football. He could simply turn and go someplace else. But he'd given his word—a promise that he'd show up. Well, okay, he'd keep his word and show up. He could always walk away whenever he wanted to.

He heard himself telling Bucky, "Yeah, I guess I'd better."

Bucky shook his head. "I wish I could see this."

"Uh-huh," Pete said. He was glad that Bucky, seriously grounded, had to go straight home from school and wouldn't be able to hang around and watch. Pete was pretty sure he was going to have Jimbo watching from the sideline. But Jimbo alone would be easier to take than the two of them egging each other on with shouts and laughs. Pete gave a little wave and walked toward the stairs leading down to the locker room.

Suddenly, with a feeling of surprise, he realized that he did not know who was on the football team. He simply had never paid attention. At the few games he had attended the previous year, he, Bucky, and Jimbo, and sometimes Rusty Lang, had had a few beers or split a half-pint of vodka and spent more time horsing around than watching the game. And, as for the pep rallies every Friday afternoon before the games, Pete and his friends had always cut out. It was easy. Nobody could take attendance at a pep rally.

Going down the stairs, Pete felt a twinge of nervousness. Then he took a deep breath and reminded himself that nothing scared Pete Holman. Nothing bothered Pete Holman. Nothing shook him. Yet...

By the time he reached the bottom of the stairs he was aware that the palms of his hands were damp with sweat. This was crazy. What was wrong? He was going to walk in there and announce that Pete Holman had arrived. Just like he always did in a new situation—he let everyone know exactly who he was. That was all. Simple. Nothing to worry about.

But now just a half dozen steps from the locker-room door, he stopped, took another deep breath, and weighed the consequences of turning around and leaving.

Then somebody walked past him into the locker room, and Pete followed him inside.

Chapter Three

"**H**i, Pete," Coach Wilson said. He seemed to have been waiting for Pete. But if he was concerned that Pete might not show up, he gave no sign. "Over here."

Pete looked around. Everywhere boys were peeling off their street clothes, working their way into shoulder pads, pulling on sweatshirts, tying shoes.

His gaze stopped on Alan Hollis. So that jerk was on the football team. It figured. Alan was smiling, and the smile froze as he caught sight of Pete. Pete consciously did not change expression—neither a smile nor a frown, just nothing—and then looked on past Alan. Pete knew that that was the best way to put somebody down. Just ignore them, don't admit they exist.

Most of the faces were familiar, from the classrooms, from the hallways. He knew some of the names, but not all.

Nobody said anything to him.

He followed Coach Wilson across to a table,

18

where a boy Pete knew from a couple of classes joined them. Pete looked at him without the first sign of recognition. Pete always made sure that others had to acknowledge him first. That way, if somebody tried to treat him like a nobody, he wasn't left with his face hanging out.

The boy said, "Hi, Pete."

Pete nodded to him.

Coach Wilson said, "Bernie is the student manager. He'll fix you up with a practice uniform and a locker. And he's going to weigh and measure you for the record." He nodded to Bernie and then turned back to Pete. "See you outside," he said, and he turned and walked away.

Pete now stared at Bernie and felt very alone. He clenched and unclenched his right fist, wishing his palms were not sweaty. "Okay," he said to Bernie, giving his best effort at the I-don't-care tone.

"Right!" Bernie announced with the same level of enthusiasm he always mustered in the classroom.

Bernie directed Pete to the scales and marked down his weight, one hundred and eighty-seven pounds. "Sound right?" he asked, and Pete nodded. He measured his height, five feet eleven, and wrote it down. Then he handed Pete a basket of clothes and said, "This way."

Pete followed Bernie toward a row of lockers, feeling foolish with the basket of clothes in his arms, doing what he was told without question—and with everyone watching. They all knew who he was; he was sure of it. That's Pete Holman, the guy who's always cutting classes, the guy who got caught smoking on school grounds. They knew him, all right, and Pete was sure of what they were thinking. And they didn't like his being here—he was sure of that, too.

Bernie stopped in front of a locker and opened the door. "Your private dressing room," he said with a laugh and a sweep of his arm. Then he was gone.

Before he thought, Pete said to Bernie's departing back, "Thanks." Then he hoped nobody had heard him.

The players were lined up in three rows in front of the goalposts at the end of the field, ten or eleven to a row. Pete was at the end of the second row. Facing them at the front was one player—Pete knew that his name was Art Tracy—leading the squad in stretching exercises.

Pete bent and stooped and twisted with the rest of them.

The early September afternoon sun was hot, and almost immediately Pete found himself dripping with perspiration. The front of his sweatshirt was wet. The sweat was running down off his forehead and into his eyes, making them sting.

Legs spread, he bent and reached across with his right hand to touch his left foot. He felt a muscle—or something—pull in the back of his right leg.

Then he stood when Art Tracy stood and, like the rest of the players, began jogging in place as Art was doing.

"I can just jog right out of here," Pete puffed to himself. "Jog right into the locker room and take off this uniform and tell Bernie to stuff it in his ear—and tell Coach Wilson the same if he's around."

Pete liked the thought, but he kept jogging in place.

Coach Wilson appeared at his side, watched for a moment, and walked on.

Pete glanced to his left and saw Alan Hollis in the row in front of him, jogging in place. Well, if Alan Hollis can do it, so can Pete Holman. He continued jogging in place. There was nothing else to do—he kept hearing in his mind Alan Hollis telling everybody, "Pete Holman couldn't take it, lasted less than an hour. Some tough guy, huh? Haw-haw-haw." Pete jogged a little faster. He was running out of breath.

Finally, it ended.

Pete was gasping, and he felt light-headed. He rubbed his eyes and wiped the sweat off his forehead. It was okay. Some of the others were doing the same thing.

He hoped Jimbo wasn't there, watching him panting and blinking and wiping the sweat away. He hadn't seen him. Maybe he hadn't shown up. Pete resisted the temptation to look around for him.

All of a sudden, everyone was going somewhere, acting like they knew what they were doing. Some were jogging off to the other end of the field. The assistant coach—Pete didn't know his name—was going with them. Other players were gathering in the middle of the field with Coach Wilson, not far in front of Pete. Where was he supposed to go? What was he supposed to do? Nobody was offering any help, and Pete just looked around.

"Over here, Pete," Coach Wilson called out.

Pete was walking toward the coach when he saw the man standing at the sideline, watching. Officer Stowell looked different out of uniform. He was wearing jeans and a yellow short-sleeved sport shirt. Without the blue uniform, he looked like anyone else. He gave Pete a wave.

Pete ducked his head and broke into a jog toward Coach Wilson, acting like he hadn't noticed Officer Stowell. So the cop was checking up on him. What would he have done if Pete hadn't been there, arrest him?

"Stand back and watch for a few minutes," Coach Wilson said to Pete.

Pete nodded. He was glad to oblige. He was still

breathing hard, and the sweat continued to pour off him.

Players formed lines on either side of Art Tracy and another boy, who took turns throwing passes to receivers crossing in front of them. Art's passes went out like a bullet and usually hit their mark. The other boy's throws wobbled and sometimes fell short. Pete had played football in neighborhood pickup games. He had caught passes. There was nothing to it. Now, watching these guys, he thought he was probably better at it than most of them.

Coach Wilson stood behind Art and the other boy, watching without saying anything, and then moved across and took a position next to Pete. "The conditioning will come," he said. "You're a week later than the others in starting practice, and you're a couple of months behind those who worked on their physical conditioning all summer."

Pete started to say, "I'm all right." But maybe it showed that he was sweating more and breathing harder than the others. So he just nodded.

"I'll give you a playbook after practice. You'll need to study it."

Pete glanced at Coach Wilson. The coach sounded like he figured Pete was out for football to stay. He nodded again.

Then, after the coach drifted away, Pete said aloud, "We'll see."

Chapter Four

The sun had almost disappeared below the horizon by the time Pete got home. He knew that his mother had left for the hospital several hours earlier. He unlocked the front door and stepped into the darkening living room. He turned on one lamp, then another, and dropped the blue ring binder notebook with a bulldog on the cover—the team's playbook—on the sofa.

Standing in the middle of the floor, he stretched his arms above his head. He felt stiff in the joints, as if he'd just awakened. And he hurt a little in some strange places, mainly his calves.

He walked into the kitchen, flipped on the light switch, and stood in front of the refrigerator reading the note his mother had left on the door, pinned by a little magnet: "Meat loaf and baked potato in fridge. Micro 1 min. Also salad. Hope football practice went well."

Normally, Pete would have shaken his head. But not this time. He was too tired.

Normally, too, he probably would have dumped the meat loaf and baked potato and gone out for a burger and fries and some laughs with the guys. He was too tired for that, too. The meat loaf didn't sound bad. Maybe later.

He opened the refrigerator door, took out a can of root beer, and walked back into the living room. He dropped onto the sofa and took a long drag on the soda. It was cold and tasted good.

So his mother hoped football practice went well. Funny how she had seemed so pleased when he told her at breakfast that he might give football a try.

He took a deep breath and glanced at the playbook by his side. He had never been so tired in his entire life.

Football practice had started badly and then had gotten worse.

First there had been the calisthenics. He'd reached a point where he could hardly breathe, and the sweat had been running off him in buckets. Maybe he should have followed his first instinct and just walked away from it right then. Good-bye, farewell, so long, and adios. He could have done it. Nobody could have stopped him.

Then after the calisthenics, when he didn't know where to go next, Coach Wilson had told him to stand around and watch. That hadn't been so bad, but it didn't last very long.

The next thing he knew, he was in the line of players running out for passes. It had all looked real easy when he was standing there with the others. He remembered snagging passes in the pickup games, and he thought these guys who dropped their passes looked pretty silly.

Yet he had caught only one of the six thrown to him. He figured it wasn't really his fault. Art Tracy threw them too hard. And the other guy who was throwing couldn't hit the side of a barn. But Coach Wilson seemed to think that some of the problem was indeed Pete's. He told him after one dropped pass, "You have to concentrate, really concentrate, to catch the ball." After another, he said, "You took your eye off the ball."

Both times, Pete answered, "Uh-huh."

Pete frowned when he recalled what Coach Wilson had said to him at the end of the passing drill: "Don't worry, you'll get the hang of it." The coach made it sound as if the whole problem was that Pete just didn't know anything about catching passes, but that maybe he could learn. That was when Pete had thought again about walking out.

Then they ran plays. Coach Wilson lined Pete up at the running back position, alternating him with Jeff Robbins, who acted like he knew what he was doing. And they ran plays—and ran them, and ran them, and ran them.

Since Pete didn't know the plays, Art Tracy, the quarterback, told him what to do in the backfield before each one. At first, Pete felt like a jerk, getting his instructions from Mr. Big Shot. It didn't help that he once spotted Jeff watching him from the side with a grin and saying something to another player. Pete came close to telling Art to shove it and walking off the field. By the end, though, he found himself wondering if maybe Art wasn't just trying to be helpful. Art Tracy did seem like a nice guy.

One good thing was that Alan Hollis was off at the other end of the field with the assistant coach, working on defense, and wasn't there to watch Pete drop passes and take directions from Art.

And then, finally, when the whole stupid thing came to an end, what did Coach Wilson do? He made everyone run up and down the field five times before going in for a shower. Pete could hardly lift his feet, and he was out of breath before the second trip up the field.

As they were trooping to the locker room, Coach Wilson called out, "Tomorrow we scrimmage, full speed, contact."

Pete knew enough about football to understand what the announcement meant—hard running and blocking against a defense that was trying to knock people down. But probably it didn't matter. Pete didn't think it was very likely he would be around to take part.

In the showers and then while getting dressed, a lot of the players horsed around and laughed and shouted at one another. Pete figured they were probably trying to act as if they weren't dead on their feet. Even if he had known any of them well enough to joke with them, he was too tired to join in.

He finally got himself dressed and walked toward the door.

"Pete," Coach Wilson called out. He was smiling in a friendly way. "Here's your playbook."

Pete looked at the blue ring binder being held out toward him. He started to say something—"I've had enough of this, and I'm out" were the words passing through his mind—but then the binder was in his hands.

"Let me explain something," Coach Wilson said.

"Huh?"

"This material is highly confidential. These are the plays we'll be running in games. It's important that this book not fall into the wrong hands. Any player who loses his playbook is suspended for at least one game."

Pete looked at the book in his hands. He thought, So what? But he said, "Okay."

"Each book is marked with the player's jersey number. Yours, you'll see, is twenty-two. That way, if a book turns up in the wrong place, it's easy to see whose it is." Coach Wilson, no longer smiling, was watching Pete. "Understand?"

Big deal, Pete thought. He said, "Uh-huh."

Pete finished off the root beer and leaned back on the sofa, staring blankly at the empty can. It felt good just to sit still. Then he glanced at his wrist-watch. Six-thirty.

He got to his feet and walked across to the telephone. He thought he should give Bucky a buzz and fill him in. He would be expecting it. He could almost hear Bucky's question: "Well, did you walk out after thirty minutes?"

Pete had his answer ready. "No way! I stayed through to the end because they were all watching me, expecting me to quit any minute. I wasn't going to give them the satisfaction." That sounded good.

He punched the buttons on the phone.

After three rings, Bucky's mother answered. "Bucky can't come to the phone," she told Pete. "He can't talk on the phone after six o'clock on school nights."

"What? I mean, why?"

"We have some new rules after what happened Saturday night."

Pete almost gave a low whistle. Bucky's parents meant business.

"Okay," he said, and hung up.

Pete considered calling Jimbo. He was curious about whether Jimbo had watched any of the practice. But he decided not to bother. By this hour, Jimbo was out somewhere, probably at the mall, and that was for sure.

Pete heated up the meat loaf and baked potato in the microwave, took another can of root beer from the refrigerator, and settled himself on a bar stool at the kitchen counter to eat and watch television.

He wondered again about Jimbo. He could probably catch up with him at the mall. Jimbo lived just a couple of blocks away from it and was there every night. But without Bucky's car, a trip to the mall for Pete meant a long walk or hitchhiking on Cartwright Avenue. The last thing in the world that Pete wanted to do right now was walk, or even stand on Cartwright Avenue with his thumb out.

Just as he was finishing the meal, the telephone rang.

"Jimbo," Pete said aloud as he slid off the bar stool and walked across to the phone. He wasn't going to have any trouble telling Jimbo to forget it tonight, unless by some miracle he had wheels.

"Hey," Pete said into the phone.

"Pete?" It wasn't Jimbo.

"Yes?"

"Officer Stowell here. How'd it go? I couldn't resist dropping around to watch for a few minutes, but I couldn't stay."

"Yeah, I saw you."

"The first day is always the toughest."

Pete waited before answering. "It wasn't so tough."

"Good. I just wanted to touch base with you, and tell you to hang in there. It'll be worth the work in the end."

Pete said nothing for a moment. Did this guy really believe that Pete Holman was going to spend the rest of his life running back and forth on a field with that bunch of jerks? Then he said, "Sure."

"Good luck, and hang in there."

"Yeah."

Pete hung up the phone slowly. He had no trouble seeing through to the motive behind the call. The cop was giving him a little reminder that he was supposed to show up for another day, and maybe at the same time he thought he was offering encouragement. Pete had seen the tactic before, usually from teachers talking about his potential. Next thing he knew, Coach Wilson would be calling to tell him how good he had looked on his first day.

Pete washed the dishes, dried them, and put

them away. Then he walked into the living room and stood in front of the sofa, looking down at the bulldog on the cover of the blue notebook. The bulldog was wearing a mean expression and a stupid-looking cap with a *C* on it.

Pete had never seen a playbook before, hadn't even known such a thing existed. Out of curiosity, he picked it up and opened it.

Then he sat down.

Maybe he ought to look it over a little bit. Then, if he did decide to show up tomorrow for practice, Art Tracy wouldn't have to tell him what to do on every play.

Chapter Five

Pete arrived at the early morning study hall without a second to spare. The minute hand on the wall clock clicked to the top—eight o'clock—as he stepped through the door.

He nodded to Mrs. Kinley. If he'd known it was her turn to take the study hall he wouldn't have been worried enough to run the last block to the school. She was nice and probably wouldn't have put him down as tardy for being a minute or two late.

Mrs. Kinley nodded back at Pete, consulted a piece of paper on her desk, and made a little mark with a pencil.

Pete looked around. There were only two other students—Bucky, of course, and a boy named Randall Powell. Pete wondered what Randall had done to warrant punishment. He walked toward Bucky.

"No, Pete," Mrs. Kinley said. "Over there, please."

Pete gave her a sheepish grin. She was separating her charges. Teachers always did. It held down whispering and note passing. Pete gave Bucky a shrug and dropped into a seat at a desk in the front of the room.

Poor Bucky, Pete thought. He was dying to know what happened at football practice. His mother wouldn't let him get the story on the telephone the night before. And now Mrs. Kinley was keeping them separated. Pete turned in his seat and grinned at Bucky. Bucky was watching him with a questioning expression on his face. Well, only an hour to go.

Turning back, Pete slumped in the seat and stared at the wall in front of him. He couldn't do his homework; he hadn't had time to get his books out of Bucky's locker. Too bad.

The blue ring binder with the bulldog on the cover was on the desk in front of him. Might as well glance at the pages. There was nothing else to do. He opened the notebook.

Sitting on the sofa in his living room the evening before, Pete had been puzzled at first glance by the X's and O's and the sweeping lines, some of them squiggly, some of them made up of dashes. But he knew enough about football to recognize the positions on the team. From there, he pieced together the meaning of the markings—a run, a pass, a block. He even recognized a couple of the plays he had run under Art's guidance. One was a blocking assignment, which had Pete running between right guard and right tackle with Art carrying the ball behind him. In the other play he remembered, he took a handoff from Art and carried the ball between right tackle and right end.

Pete was still leafing through the pages of the ring binder when the bell rang, startling him. He glanced at the clock on the wall—nine o'clock. Time for the first class. The hour had flown by.

Pete clapped the ring binder shut and got to his feet. He turned to Mrs. Kinley, smiled, and said very politely, "Good-bye, ma'am." She was one of the few teachers Pete liked. She always seemed nice. Mrs. Kinley smiled back.

Almost instantly, Bucky was at Pete's side, and they walked together toward the door.

"What happened?" Bucky asked.

Pete started to reply as they went through the doorway. Then he stopped. He was staring into the face of Coach Wilson.

"Let me walk with you, Pete," the coach said.

Pete frowned. He was about to ask, "What for?" But he changed his mind. He turned to Bucky and said, "See you later, okay?"

Bucky gaped at Pete for a moment. Then he mumbled something that sounded like "Sure" and left.

"Where's your class, Pete?"

Pete nodded down the hallway in the direction of Bucky's departing back. "Mrs. Ford," he said.

"Okay."

Then Pete remembered that he didn't have his books. "I have to stop by my locker," he said. It was Bucky's locker, really, but that was none of the coach's business. "It's on the way."

They began walking.

"Pete, the members of the football team do not get themselves assigned to the early morning study hall for any reason whatsoever."

Pete didn't answer. Who did this guy think he was? Pete had cut a class, gotten caught, taken the punishment. So what? Then he said, "How did you know I was there?"

"I receive a list each afternoon—it's waiting for me after practice—with the names of students assigned to the early morning study hall. I want to know if any of my players are on the list. I saw your name."

There was something about the coach's words that Pete did not like. He was roping him in with "my players." He was trying to tell Pete how he was supposed to behave. His tone, as much as his words, made it sound as if everything was settled, done, finished—Pete was a member of the football team.

Pete said, "There's my locker."

He moved away from the coach, heading across

the hallway toward the locker. He was hoping that Coach Wilson would go away now that he'd delivered his speech.

But the coach followed Pete to the row of lockers. He stood there, not saying a word, while Pete twirled the combination, opened the door, lifted out books, closed the door, and turned back around. Pete realized he still had the playbook in his stack of books. He had meant to dump it off in the locker.

Coach Wilson resumed walking toward Mrs. Ford's classroom. Pete walked with him. He had no choice.

"Normally," the coach said, "if a member of the team is assigned to the early morning study hall, he has to run an extra five laps after practice."

Pete almost gulped. Five more laps! If he decided to show up for today's football practice—and he wasn't sure he was going to—the idea of five extra laps was horrifying. As it was, he had been dead on his feet at the end of yesterday's practice.

He told himself that Pete Holman did not have to run laps for anyone. And he did not have to play football. He could do what he wanted, not what somebody said he had to do. He could look at the coach right now and announce that he was quitting. He'd tried it, as promised. He didn't like it. And now he was going his own way. So long.

But before Pete could say anything, the coach

was talking again. "But in this case, I'll excuse you," Coach Wilson said. "Technically you weren't a member of the football team when you cut that study hall, and you didn't know about my rule."

Pete, staring straight ahead, said to himself, "Well, thank *you*."

Coach Wilson was still talking. "But you're a member of the team now, and you know the rule— and you'll be running laps if your name turns up on that list again."

A member of the team? The rule? Laps? What was this guy talking about?

Coach Wilson stopped. "Here's Mrs. Ford's class."

Pete looked at him. The coach was smiling.

"Uh, yeah," Pete managed to say.

"A deal?" Coach Wilson said.

Pete just wanted to get away. He nodded and said, "Yeah, okay."

Pete turned and walked into the classroom, muttering, "I think I must be going crazy."

Mrs. Ford, standing alongside her desk, said, "What did you say, Pete?"

Pete shook his head. "Nothing. Nothing at all."

At noon, finally, Bucky was going to get filled in.

Coming out of the line in the cafeteria with a tray of food in his hands, Pete saw Bucky, Jimbo, and

Rusty Lang seated at one of the long tables. Bucky waved. Pete nodded and walked in their direction.

Jimbo greeted him with, "So, ol' Pete's going to be a football star."

Pete scowled at Jimbo. Jimbo had a way about him sometimes that made Pete want to mash his face in. And this was one of those times. He put his tray on the table and sat down.

"I watched you for a while," Jimbo said.

"Oh, yeah? I didn't see you."

"I didn't stick around long. I had better things to do."

Pete looked at Jimbo but didn't respond.

Bucky looked from Jimbo to Pete. Obviously, Pete had not turned and walked off the field after a few minutes. "Did you stay through the whole practice?"

"Yeah."

"I thought you were going to give it a half hour and then blow it off." There was nothing accusatory in Bucky's tone, as there would have been if Jimbo had been the one talking. Bucky was just curious, and maybe a little disappointed. It would have been fun to hear how Pete had walked out.

Pete recalled the line he had planned to give Bucky on the telephone the night before: Everybody was watching him, waiting for him to quit, and he decided not to give the jocks the satisfaction. The line had sounded good then for some reason, but it didn't now.

"I decided to stick it out," Pete said. Then he added, "There wasn't anything else I had to do—so why not?"

"Anyone say anything?"

Pete knew what Bucky was asking. The members of the football team lived in a different world from Pete, Bucky, and their friends. Had anyone told Pete he was in the wrong place, with the wrong people?

"Nah, nobody said anything."

Pete remembered Art Tracy helping him with the plays. That was somebody saying something. But Pete figured that wasn't the kind of thing Bucky was asking about. Besides, Jimbo was sure to pounce on any admission by Pete that he'd accepted help from the quarterback.

To Pete's surprise, Jimbo asked, "What'd Coach Wilson want with you this morning?"

Of course, Bucky would have told Jimbo that the coach had been waiting outside the early morning study hall for him.

Pete took a bite before answering. He had had a lot of experience with lying—to teachers, occasionally to the police, sometimes to his mother, and once in a while to his friends. So he lied. "He'd given me a playbook after practice and wanted to know if I had any questions."

Bucky was watching Pete. He knew he was lying. That was for sure. But he wasn't going to accuse him. Jimbo was wearing that leering grin of his. He, too, might know that Pete wasn't telling the truth. But Jimbo didn't say anything either. Rusty was concentrating on lunch. Pete looked at them and decided he didn't care if they knew he was lying. The conversation with the coach was none of their business.

Bucky asked, "Are you going back today?"

"I haven't decided."

That one reduced them to silence. Jimbo looked like he wanted to say something, then changed his mind. Pete, tired of the cross-examination, looked at Bucky and said, "I tried to call you last night."

Bucky shrugged. "Yeah, I know."

"They're not even letting you talk on the phone?"

"Not after six o'clock on school nights."

Jimbo chimed in, "Yeah, Bucky's bought heavy duty."

"What about weekends?"

"I can stay out until ten o'clock. But no car."

"No car for how long?"

"Yeah, that was what I asked my father—how long?"

"What'd he say?"

"He said I might never see the inside of the car again. And the worst part was that he wasn't shouting. He just said it, you know, like he meant it."

Jimbo shoved his tray back and got to his feet. "I'm going out for a smoke. Anybody else?"

"Sure," Bucky said.

Rusty said, "Mr. Hodges is going to come out of that boiler room one of these days and catch you guys."

Jimbo grinned at Rusty and turned to Pete. "You coming?"

Three words began whirling around in Pete's mind: five extra laps.

"You go ahead," Pete said. "I'm not finished with my lunch."

Chapter Six

After the bell ending the last class, Pete stood up and felt again the stiffness and occasional twinge of soreness in his muscles, as he had all day. Each time it was a reminder that a second day of football practice lay before him—if he chose to show up. He knew he didn't have to show up. He could just walk out of the school and head for home. He knew also that today was sure to be worse than yesterday, with full-speed scrimmaging on the schedule.

But when he stepped out of the classroom and into the hallway, he turned left and walked toward the flight of stairs leading down to the locker room.

"Let's see what happens," he said to himself.

He walked along the hallway and down the stairs to the locker room without meeting Bucky, Jimbo, or Rusty, and he was glad. They were certain to ask if he was going to report for practice again. Probably they had already figured out the answer for themselves. But they would ask anyway, just to make Pete say it. And even though Pete knew he was going to practice, he didn't want to admit it, to say it out loud.

The room was again crowded with players changing clothes. But this time there was a strange kind of quiet, with none of the chatter and laughter that had followed practice the day before. Everyone seemed, well, businesslike. Nobody gave Pete more than a glance.

Across the room, Coach Wilson was checking something with Bernie. Neither of them even looked in Pete's direction.

Pete walked to his locker, opened it, dropped his books into the bottom, and began unbuttoning his shirt.

"One more day won't matter," he said to himself.

The thought had barely passed through his mind when a voice to his left said, "Hey, Pete." He turned to face Art Tracy. What did he want?

"Did you have a chance to look through the playbook?" Art asked.

So the quarterback had seen Coach Wilson give him a playbook. Well, so what? Pete said, "Yeah, some."

"Good. The coach is going to run us through a full-speed scrimmage this afternoon. Nobody expects you to know all the plays. So when you're in there, I'll tell you what to do, or you ask me if you don't understand. Okay?"

Pete nodded. "Yeah." Then he surprised himself by adding, "Thanks."

"You'll do fine. Jeff will be on the field most of the time, but you'll probably see some action."

"Jeff?"

"Jeff Robbins. He's more than likely going to be the starting running back, as well as the punter. Same as last year." Then Art grinned and added, "Running back—that's the position Coach Wilson had you working yesterday."

"Yeah."

Pete stood in the row of players at the sideline as Coach Wilson placed the ball on the hash mark of the forty-yard line and stepped back.

Art and the offense huddled with Coach Wilson, standing off to the side. Across the forty-yard line, the defensive players settled into position, with Coach Barnett just behind them.

Pete watched Jeff Robbins. He was a senior, same as Pete, and they were about the same size. Pete knew Jeff from classes together, but nothing else. He tried to remember if he'd even known that Jeff was a football player. He wasn't sure.

On the first play, Art barked the signals, took the snap from center, turned, and spun a pitchout to Jeff. Jeff gathered in the ball, then cut sharply and plunged between tackle and end on the right side of the line. There was a lot of grunting and the thumping sounds of people running into one another. Jeff gained about four yards. Pete thought he remembered the play from the playbook.

As the scrimmage progressed—a pass, a quarterback keeper, a handoff to the fullback—Coach Wilson moved around, watching. Sometimes he leaned into the huddle and seemed to be telling Art which play to call. Other times it looked as if the coach was just listening. After a half dozen plays, he began inserting other players into the action.

Pete wondered when his turn would come. Then he heard—"Holman for Robbins!"

Pete pulled on his helmet. He wanted to look around and see if Jimbo was standing somewhere, watching, but he didn't. He snapped the helmet strap and ran onto the field, passing Jeff coming off.

In the huddle, Art looked at Pete. "Same play we walked through yesterday, with you taking a handoff and going off right tackle. Remember?"

Coach Wilson's head was in the huddle, but he didn't say anything.

Pete nodded at Art.

Art broke the huddle, and the players lined up. Pete was alone in the backfield behind Art—too far behind Art, it seemed, because Art turned to him and said, "One step closer." Pete nodded and took the step forward, then bent with hands on his knees and waited.

Two players were out wide, one to the left and one to the right. Pete remembered that the player out wide to the right was supposed to run across and block a defensive back—if Pete got that far.

Coach Wilson backed away and stood with arms folded, watching.

Art took the ball from the center, turned, moved backward, and extended the ball to Pete.

Pete lunged forward, taking the ball in both hands. Okay so far. Then he looked ahead of him— a tangle of flailing arms and straining legs, wall-to-wall players. Where was the hole? All of the diagrams in the playbook showed offensive linemen neatly shoving aside defensive linemen to create a gap for the ballcarrier. Pete could not even tell where the hole between tackle and end was supposed to be.

The picture flashed through Pete's mind in a second, and he slammed on the brakes. No point in running into a solid wall of struggling players. He took a little leap to his left. He saw a small slice of space between two players. He ran for it.

The space widened and then narrowed as Pete threw himself into it.

Somebody bumped a hip, then somebody bumped the other thigh.

But nobody grabbed him, and Pete crashed through the line, still on his feet and running.

Somebody got a hand on him just as he was veering to his left, trying to run wide to get away from the crowd of players near the middle of the field. The hand slipped away.

Pete saw nothing but empty space all the way in front of him to the goalposts—all right!

Then, so quickly that he didn't realize what was happening, he hit the ground. His feet had been tied together. He couldn't run.

He looked at his feet and saw, of all people, Alan Hollis, with his arms wrapped around Pete's ankles.

Alan let go and scrambled to his feet. He gave Pete a brief look—seeming to say, "So there, tough guy"—and turned and walked away.

Pete got up and looked back, counting the chalked yardage lines—five yards, ten, fifteen, a little more than fifteen yards gained. Maybe seventeen yards. His first thought was, How did I do that? His second thought almost put a smile on his face: That showed these jerks something, didn't it?

Somebody off to his left shouted, "Nice running," and Pete acknowledged him with a nod. Then he ducked his head and ran back to the huddle.

As he approached, he saw Coach Wilson standing back, his arms folded over his chest, watching him. The coach had a strange expression on his face. He wasn't smiling at the long run. Maybe he was angry at Pete for not running where the play dictated. But he wasn't frowning, either. It was as if he was seeing Pete for the first time.

By the end of the scrimmage Pete had carried the ball six times.

There were no more long gains, but he picked up four to seven yards on his carries. Not once was he thrown for a loss, and not once did he fumble. He had one pass thrown to him, and he dropped it.

Mostly, Pete blocked, and not well. Time and again, Coach Wilson came running up to him, shouting, "No, no, not that way—this way," and then went through the motions of blocking an imaginary tackler.

Every time he carried the ball, and every time he struggled to make a block, Pete asked himself, What am I doing? But then his memory would replay the electric thrill he felt when he ran into that small opening in the line and crashed through, running free.

Near the finish, Pete caught himself comparing his performance with Jeff Robbins's. The idea immediately set off alarm bells in his mind. What do I care? What does it matter? Then he took another handoff or lunged forward for another block.

While Pete was running wind sprints at the end of practice, Jimbo came back into his mind. Pete looked around. No Jimbo in sight.

But Pete did see a familiar figure on the sideline. Officer Stowell, in uniform this time, was standing with Coach Wilson down near the goal line.

They seemed to be looking at him. Maybe they were talking about him.

Well, so what?

The lights were on in the living room when Pete approached his house, reminding him that this was Tuesday, the first of his mother's two off-duty nights each week. Tuesday evening had slipped up on him. Things had been pretty busy the last couple of days.

He cut across the yard and headed for the door, recalling his misery coming home the evening before. He was tired now, but not as bone weary as he had been at the end of the first practice, and there seemed to be less of the stiffness. Maybe the exertion got easier to take as things went along. Probably so. But he was wearing something new tonight—a bruise on his thigh that made itself known with each step.

"Well, it's Mr. Touchdown." His mother greeted him with a smile. "How did it go today?"

"Okay, I guess."

"C'mon in the kitchen. Dinner is just a few minutes away."

Pete dropped his books onto the sofa and followed his mother into the kitchen.

"When is the first game?" she asked.

Pete looked at his mother. She was assuming that he was on the football team to stay. She didn't know what had led to his signing up in the first place. And she didn't know how many times in two days he had almost chucked it all—and that he still might.

"A week from Friday," he said finally. "Windham High."

Chapter Seven

By the end of the practice week, Pete was still showing up every day, working out with the team, showering, and going home.

That's not to say he wasn't puzzled by this new pattern in his life. Straining through the calisthenics opening each practice session, adding new bruises in the daily scrimmages, puffing through the wind sprints at the end of practice, he kept asking himself, Why?

In scrimmages, Pete ran wild through the field full of players twice more, once going all forty yards to the goal line. In both of the long runs he found his planned route blocked and, leaping around, found another way to go.

Each time, he looked around with amazement: Look what I did! Once he waved at someone who shouted, "Great run!" And he noticed Coach Wilson, arms folded over his chest, watching him in that funny way.

After four failures as a pass receiver, Pete finally

caught—and held on to—one of Art Tracy's zinging throws. It was a play that had Pete drifting out to the right while Art went through all sorts of fancy faking. Then Pete broke into a run down the sideline and Art passed to him. It didn't matter that a linebacker saw what was developing and immediately arrived and slammed Pete to the ground. Pete held on to the ball.

He even laid a perfectly executed block on a defensive lineman, opening a hole for the fullback, Kevin Hughes, to run through. On that one, Coach Wilson called out, "Nice block," and Art, returning to the huddle, gave Pete a one-armed hug of congratulations.

Gradually, he began to think he knew the answer when he asked himself why he kept coming back.

Off the practice field, Pete found himself studying the playbook in his spare time in study hall and at home. At first, this puzzled him, too. Nobody had ever called Pete Holman studious. He put in the time needed on his studies to get by but nothing more. Sure, he had worked hard on chemistry once for a while. The idea of elements mixing together and creating something new had fascinated him. But not for long. It soon became drudgery—too much work—and his interest had faded away. It was no longer fun. But Pete's interest in the playbook did not fade away. Before long, he was sure he knew the plays as well as anyone, and the confidence felt good. He was mastering something that—strangely— seemed to matter.

He knew he could never explain this to his friends, and he didn't try.

For Bucky, Jimbo, and Rusty, a good time was a couple of beers or a half-pint of vodka, and something to be mastered meant spray painting a wall. None of them had ever run to the end zone, caught an Art Tracy bullet pass, thrown a block.

No, they'd never understand.

Besides, these days his time with Bucky, Jimbo, and Rusty was mostly confined to the lunch period. Football practice was not only taking up the afternoons but was also leaving him too weary in the evenings for hanging around the mall. Especially since Bucky no longer had the wheels to move them around.

Sometimes at lunch Pete would glance across at the tables where the football players were gathered. He wondered how they would act if he sat down with them one day. He wondered, too, what Jimbo would say. Plenty, for sure. So he kept eating with his friends, going along with their jokes, their gripes about teachers, and Bucky's constant moaning about being grounded. Pete never mentioned football to them, and they seldom brought it up.

At lunch on Friday, Pete was sitting across from

Jimbo when Jimbo methodically lined up three green peas on the table. It was a favorite stunt of Jimbo's—cocking his middle finger on his thumb, then releasing and sending a green pea rocketing toward another table. If it hit somebody—great! Even if not, it was sure to startle somebody. Either way, a real yuk for Jimbo and his friends.

But Pete found himself saying, "For crying out loud, Jimbo."

Jimbo fired a pea. It didn't hit anyone, but a girl at the next table turned and looked.

"Quit it," Pete said. Beyond Jimbo, Pete saw Alan Hollis say something to Art Tracy, and Art turned and watched. So did a couple of the other players.

Jimbo cocked and fired again—another miss and another sharp look from the girl at the next table.

Jimbo laughed.

Pete put his hand over Jimbo's. "That's enough. If you don't quit, I'm moving."

Bucky looked like he was starting to laugh, but then stopped and watched Pete.

"Going to go sit with the jocks?" Jimbo said.

"Maybe. That way, I won't have people at my table embarrassing me."

Jimbo stared at Pete a moment, then went back to eating his lunch without firing the third green pea.

After a moment of awkward silence, Bucky

turned to Pete and asked, "Do you like it?" He sort of underlined the word *like* to give it a tone of disbelief. He didn't mention football, but his meaning was clear.

"Some of it is fun," Pete answered without committing himself.

Bucky shook his head. "Boy, all of a sudden everything sure is different. Here I am, grounded—and I may never get the car again. And there you are, running your tail off with a bunch of jocks. I never thought I'd see you…"

Bucky let the sentence trail off, and Pete let the comment go unanswered. They wouldn't understand the incredible thrill he felt every time he succeeded on the football field—making a good run, catching a pass, making a block. So he didn't even try to tell them.

But Jimbo saw something in Pete's face, or heard something in his silence, because he told Bucky, "Too bad you're grounded and can't stay after school to watch football practice. I've watched a couple of times. It's something to see. You wouldn't believe it, Bucky."

Pete had the beginnings of a frown on his face. He'd heard this kind of routine from Jimbo before.

Bucky looked at Jimbo. "Believe what?"

"Our old buddy, out there with the jocks."

"Cut it out," Pete said.

"He's trying to be one of them, you know, doing what he's told, just like all the rest of them. You wouldn't believe it."

Bucky watched Pete.

"I said, cut it out," Pete snapped.

Jimbo kept his smile aimed at Pete, nodded, and said nothing, satisfied that his needling had forced a response.

When they finished eating, Bucky shoved his tray to the side and said, "Let's go out for a smoke."

"Don't you remember, Bucky? Pete doesn't smoke anymore," Jimbo said.

Pete glared at him. In truth, he hadn't actually quit, hadn't made a grand pronouncement that he was through with cigarettes. But he had not smoked since Monday morning, when he and Bucky cut their study hall. He had come out of the first day of practice wondering if cigarette smoking was part of his trouble trying to get his breath after the wind sprints. In the following days, he simply hadn't smoked, and he had ducked the invitations to join Bucky and Jimbo and some of the others outside the boiler room.

"Have you quit?" Bucky asked.

Pete said only, "Not necessarily."

"Then c'mon."

Pete remembered, too, Coach Wilson's penalty for being assigned to early morning study hall—and that was sure to happen one day when Mr. Hodges suddenly opened the door from the boiler room.

"You guys go ahead. I've got to study this playbook."

Jimbo stood, looked at Pete for a moment, and then picked up the playbook from the table and flipped through the pages. "All the secret plays of the mighty Cartwright High Bulldogs, eh?"

"Something like that," Pete said, taking the playbook away from Jimbo and closing it with a snap.

He didn't open it again until Jimbo and Bucky were out of the cafeteria.

Chapter Eight

Pete stepped out of the back door of the school, his hair still wet from the shower following the Saturday morning drill, and stood for a moment in the noon-hour sunshine.

One week, he thought to himself. It's been one week. At this time a week ago, he was looking forward to a night of fun with Bucky, Jimbo, and some of the others. A few beers, some jokes, the usual. Football never once entered his mind. But now he had struggled through six practice sessions.

"See you Monday," somebody said, and Pete turned to see Tucker Williamson, a wide receiver, walking past and waving.

"Yeah," Pete called back to him with a wave.

Beyond Tucker he saw Alan Hollis and Jeff Robbins walking together toward a car. Jeff noticed Pete watching them and gave a little wave. Alan turned to see who Jeff was waving at. He looked at Pete, and then turned back to Jeff, saying something.

Pete shrugged and started to walk toward home.

He was looking forward to lunch. Four hours of pounding the turf on the practice field—running, blocking, bumping, struggling with tacklers—had burned up breakfast in a hurry. He was hungry.

"Hey, Pete—wait up."

Pete turned and saw Art Tracy approaching from the side. Pete stopped and Art fell in step with him.

"You got anything on tonight?"

Pete started to say that he did. Although nothing was set, Jimbo and some of the guys were sure to be expecting Pete to join them.

Pete said to Art, "Nothing definite. Why?"

"Some of us are going over to Brookfield High. They're having a battle of the bands. A group from Cartwright High is going to be there. Want to come along?"

Pete looked at Art. He didn't know what to say.

"It ought to be pretty good," Art added.

"Yeah, okay," Pete said. "Sounds good."

"Great. We'll pick you up about six. Okay?"

"Fine," Pete said. Then it occurred to Pete that neither Art nor any of his friends had any reason to know where he lived, and he gave Art his address.

"See you then," Art said, and peeled off to the right.

Pete stared after him. The quarterback had been friendly and helpful from the beginning. To Pete, this had been puzzling. The jocks weren't supposed to be friendly and helpful, except to one another, right? Then why was Art so nice to him when he suddenly appeared on the football field?

Pete also wondered who the "some of us" might be who were going to the battle of the bands. Football players, probably. So this was what the jocks did on a Saturday night. Pete almost smiled to himself. No beer, no cigarettes—not with that bunch. And not at Brookfield High.

Pete reflected that this Saturday night was going to be very different from last week's. He ended *that* Saturday night in the police station. This week he'd be spending Saturday evening at, of all places, a school!

Pete's mother had lunch on the table when he got home. He got a can of root beer out of the refrigerator and wasted no time devouring two sandwiches.

"Hard practice?" his mother asked.

Pete nodded while chewing the last bite, swallowed, and said, "Hard."

Beth Holman scooped up the plates and took them into the kitchen, and Pete followed her with their glasses, placing them on the counter. He walked into the living room, wondering what he was going to say when Jimbo or Bucky called.

He sat on the sofa, picked up the Cartwright *Morning Herald,* and glanced at it.

His mother was coming into the living room when she looked out the window and said, "There's a police car pulling up in front."

"Huh?" Pete got up to join her at the window. He watched the lone uniformed officer in the car step out.

"That's Officer Stowell," Pete said.

"Oh?"

His mother's tone spoke volumes. Pete had never been involved in any really serious trouble with the police, but he had skirted around the edges for a while. His mother was used to receiving notices from the school about his cutting classes and his smoking cigarettes on the school grounds. And she didn't like the looks of Jimbo, and told Pete so often enough. So she certainly might think that a visit by a police officer wasn't just a social call.

"He's a friend of Coach Wilson's," Pete said. "He played for the Bulldogs when he was at Cartwright High, and he comes by to watch practice sometimes."

"Oh." The tone changed.

"I'll see what he wants."

Pete stepped out the front door and gave Officer Stowell a little wave. The man had been nice to him at the police station last Saturday night. He did not fit Pete's idea of what a policeman was supposed to act like, and Pete found himself wondering from time to time why the officer had gone out of his way to help him. Pete said, "Hi."

"Good afternoon, Pete." Officer Stowell spoke with businesslike briskness that set off a tiny alarm bell in Pete's mind. Had Jimbo and some of the guys swallowed a few beers the night before and spray painted a wall or something? It was possible. And was Officer Stowell here to ask if Pete had been with them? A reasonable question, maybe. In fact, Pete had spent Friday night at home, ducking Jimbo's invitation with a plea that he needed a good night's rest before the Saturday morning practice. But still, Pete didn't relish being questioned about whatever might have happened.

Then Officer Stowell, stepping onto the small front porch, smiled and said, "I'm glad I've caught you at home, Pete."

Pete returned the smile with a feeling of relief, ushered the officer into the house, and asked, "Would you like a root beer or anything?"

"Thanks, no. I can't stay long. I'm on patrol duty. But I did want to talk to you."

"Oh?" Pete's smile faded, and he was frowning as he led the way through the living room toward the deck.

Here comes another lecture. Pete dreaded the idea. He'd heard it all before—the bad influence of the wrong friends, failure to measure up to potential, all the missed opportunities, blah, blah, blah. Even worse, he dreaded a lecture here on the deck, where his mother might walk into the middle of the conversation. Then she'd find out that he had been hauled in by the police last weekend after Bucky smashed into that parked car.

They sat across from each other at the redwood picnic table at the edge of the deck.

"You've finished a week of football practice," Officer Stowell began.

"Uh-huh."

"Frankly, a week ago tonight neither Coach Wilson nor I was sure that you would do it."

Pete couldn't help smiling. "Neither was I," he said.

Officer Stowell did not return the smile. "Every day since then, I've wondered if you were going to show up again. And I think Coach Wilson was wondering, too."

The officer paused, clearly waiting for Pete to speak. But Pete retreated back into his usual wait-and-see silence.

"I watched practice a couple of days this week."

"Yeah, I saw you."

"My eyes nearly popped out of my head on

Tuesday when you shifted gears and found that hole in the line." He shook his head in disbelief. "Seventeen yards," he said.

Pete smiled at the memory.

"You're a natural," Officer Stowell said.

"Huh?"

"There isn't a coach in the world who can teach a runner to do that. He can either do it or he can't. It's as simple as that. And very few runners can do it."

Pete did not speak. He wasn't used to this kind of praise. Was this guy in a police uniform trying to con him? If so, why? What was in it for him? As a matter of fact, what had been in it for him from the beginning?

"You took a play that was going nowhere—there was no hole in the line where it was supposed to be. And on instinct you turned and ran where there was one."

Pete didn't know what to say. He rubbed his chin. Finally he said guardedly, "A natural, huh? Sounds pretty good."

"It is. Coach Wilson told me that you did it a couple of other times later in the week. So it wasn't a fluke. It'd be a big mistake if you decided to quit," Officer Stowell continued. "You've got tremendous potential."

Oh, no! Pete almost groaned out loud. *Potential!*

Here's that word again. And here comes another "lost potential" lecture! You really had me going for a minute, cop.

Pete stared past Officer Stowell, waiting for the man to begin, waiting to tune him out.

But Officer Stowell didn't keep talking. He just watched Pete.

In the silence that followed, Pete shifted on the bench. Finally, he looked at Officer Stowell and said, "What's the deal? Why are you doing all this for me? Why did you call Coach Wilson to sign me out of the police station, then team up with him to get me to go out for the football team? And why did you come by practice to watch me and now to tell me how good I am? I don't get it. Nobody does anything for nothing."

Officer Stowell looked at Pete and then let his gaze wander to a point beyond him. Pete thought once that he was about to answer, but then he remained silent, as if thinking better of what he was going to say.

Finally, he smiled and said, "I thought you looked like a football player the moment I saw you. That was a pretty good move you put on me in the street after the accident, you know. You've got the build for football. You walked like a football player. You even stood still like a football player, if that's possible. So I asked myself, why isn't this boy a football player?"

Pete frowned at Officer Stowell's smile. Maybe he was telling the truth. But it seemed too simple, too pat. He said, "So you're just a recruiter for the Bulldogs."

"There's more to it than that." The officer's smile was gone. "I watch the kids brought in on Friday and Saturday nights—for vandalism, drunkenness, pot, all of that. Our standard procedure is to call the parents. When the parents come to get them, they're always angry—angry at their kids and sometimes also at us. They blame the police for causing all the trouble and embarrassment. We send the kids home with their parents—and the same ones are back again in a week or two."

In his mind, Pete saw Bucky's face, Jimbo's—and his own.

"So when I saw you, I thought, let's try something a little different, and Coach Wilson agreed to go along with me."

"I see. I'm an experiment."

Officer Stowell smiled. "Maybe," he said. Then the smile stopped. "Whether or not you're an experiment isn't important. What is important is that you hang in there and make this thing work—for your own good."

Pete nodded, but that was all.

Officer Stowell said, "Well, I've said what I came to say. I've got to get back on patrol." He got to his feet.

Pete stood up with him.

He was alone in the house.

Officer Stowell had left a half hour earlier. Pete had walked with him to his patrol car, then had waved as the policeman drove away.

His mother had left for the hospital shortly after. Pete had successfully turned back her inquiries about Officer Stowell's visit by saying, "He's a Bulldogs fan."

In the quiet of the empty house, Pete stood at the front window, hands poked into the pockets of his jeans, and stared out. Then he turned and walked across to the sofa and sat down.

He heard again the words of Officer Stowell— "You're a natural"—and he gave a little smile and shook his head slightly. Maybe, just maybe, Officer Stowell was a nice guy who was saying something that was important to Pete Holman.

Pete had to admit that there were moments of fun and excitement in football. Oh, there were the bruises, the creaking muscles, and the sweat, always a lot of sweat. But there was the thrill of taking a handoff, finding a hole in the line, running through it, spinning away from a tackler. Who would ever have thought Pete Holman could do it?

For the first time, Pete saw signs of new friend-ships. Art Tracy had been friendly from the begin-ning. So had some others, now that Pete thought about it. They helped him with the plays and cheered his runs. Tonight he was going to the battle of the bands with Art and some others.

It was a whole new world, and he knew now that it was his to have if—

If he chose to take it.

"I'll stick it out," he said aloud.

When the telephone rang, Pete did not an-swer it.

Chapter Nine

When Pete arrived at school on Monday morning the huge banner was stretched across the wall in the lobby—blue letters on a field of white: BEAT WINDHAM.

Pete had seen the banners before, every week of football season, exhorting the Bulldogs to beat the team coming up on the schedule that Friday night.

He'd never paid any attention to them before. Who cared which team the Bulldogs were playing? And who cared who won?

But this time he stopped and stared at the banner for a moment. It was a reminder that the first game of the season was four days away. And that he was going to be part of that game.

Pete walked on toward his locker. The hallway was full of students, some arriving and heading for their lockers, others chatting in groups near their first class. He didn't greet many of them. He knew them, sure, and they knew him, but that was as far as it went.

Turning a corner, he looked down the hallway toward his locker and spotted Bucky standing in front of it with the door open. He was rummaging around on the top shelf of Pete's locker. Then Bucky stepped back, stared into the locker a moment, and closed the door as Pete approached.

"What's up?" Pete asked.

Bucky turned. "I was looking for a smoke." He grinned. "There's just time left for a quickie before the bell rings. I thought maybe you had some left in your locker."

"I don't think so."

"Nope, nothing. You've really quit, huh?"

"Sort of. Maybe Jimbo—is he around?"

"Jimbo's never got his own smokes. You know that."

Pete stepped in front of the locker and began turning the dial on the combination lock.

"I'll find somebody," Bucky said, walking away. "See you later."

"Yeah."

Pete opened the locker and felt relieved that Bucky had left and Jimbo was nowhere in sight. He did not need a rerun of Sunday afternoon. He had let the telephone ring unanswered twice on Saturday afternoon. In the wake of the conversation with Officer Stowell, Pete had not felt like bumming around with Jimbo and Bucky at the mall. Then later, in the early evening, he was glad to get into Art Tracy's car and put himself beyond reach of the telephone. But all through the battle of the bands and pizza afterward—a really good time—he knew that he was going to have to talk to Jimbo and Bucky sometime. And on Sunday afternoon he did.

His mother called him in from cutting the grass to take the telephone call.

"Where've you been, man?" The voice was Jimbo's.

Pete took a deep breath. "You mean yesterday?"

"Well, yeah, for starters."

"I had football practice in the morning."

"I know that, man." Jimbo's voice was taking on an accusatory tone. "But Bucky tried to call you in the afternoon, and then both of us called later from the mall. There wasn't any answer. We were looking for you."

"I guess I was outside."

Jimbo did not speak.

"Look," Pete said finally. "I was beat, and I just lay around the house."

The line was silent for a moment. Then Jimbo said, "Well, I'm at the mall now, and Bucky and Rusty are on the way. You coming?"

"I've got to finish the grass."

◆　◆　◆　◆　◆

The Monday afternoon practice was light—no scrimmaging—and the emphasis was on executing plays. "A signals drill," Art Tracy called it.

From the first stooping motion at the start of calisthenics to the final wind sprint that ended the practice session, Pete compared what was happening with the events of his first day, just one week ago. The calisthenics were easier this time. For sure, he was sweating in the heat of the early autumn sunshine, but the sweat was not pouring off him in torrents, as it had on that first day. And he still felt the occasional twinge in a muscle being stretched. But it felt sort of good now, not painful. Following the calisthenics, he knew where to go on the practice field and what to do. When they ran plays, he knew his role and no longer had to turn a puzzled expression to Art for directions. And this time he did not once consider the possibility of turning and walking away. This time he wondered about taking the field against the Windham High Bobcats with a large crowd of people watching. The prospect made him concentrate all the harder. He did not want to make a dumb mistake in a game.

Then on Tuesday the Bulldogs went back to hard work—a full-speed scrimmage—but with a difference: Pete was in the backfield for more plays than on any of the scrimmage days last week. Jeff

Robbins spent a little less time on the field—about the same amount of time that Pete put in—and Larry Helm got into action for only three plays.

All through the Tuesday scrimmage, and again in Wednesday's scrimmage, Pete increasingly found his way blocked when he leaped to the side to find his own hole in the line. The defenders had become wary of him, cautious about committing themselves to the path he seemed to be taking. They waited— just for the blink of an eye, but it was still a delay— to see if he was going to shift direction.

Art saw what was happening and told Pete, "Don't worry, it'll balance out. If they're hanging back to see which way you're going to run, it means you've got easier running in the original hole in the line."

In his time on the sideline, Pete watched Jeff on the field. Jeff was as strong as Pete, maybe stronger, and he was almost as fast. He was not as quick as Pete in changing direction, and Pete saw that as an important plus for him. But Jeff had a big advantage in experience. Jeff was playing his third year of var-sity football. He had been absorbing instruction and learning by doing for three years. Pete had never carried the ball in a real game. Pete knew that the difference showed.

So Pete knew the answer when Bucky asked on Friday morning while they walked to Mrs.

Chisholm's classroom, "Are you going to be starting the game?"

"I don't think so," he said.

Pete stood on the stage in the auditorium with the other players and stared out at the crowd of cheering, shouting students. A pep band blared and pounded away, adding to the deafening noise and general sense of chaos.

Eight cheerleaders were lined up at the front of the stage, whirling and pumping their fists into the air, leading the shouting.

Gazing at the scene before him, Pete reflected that he was attending a pep rally for the first time. He, Bucky, Jimbo, and some of the others always cut out, happy that they were legally out of the last class, if illegally missing from the pep rally. Pete almost grinned at the thought.

He looked at the crowd and wondered if Bucky and Jimbo were there—attending to see their old friend Pete up there on the stage with the jocks, one of them. Probably not, Pete decided.

Alongside Pete, some of the players were wearing letter jackets of bright blue with a large white *C* stitched on the left breast. Some of them grinned and joked nervously, while others stood rigidly self-conscious.

Pete, wearing a red, gray, and white rugby shirt and jeans, stood with his hands stuffed in his pockets and watched the scene in front of him.

Some of the faces in the crowd were pointed at Pete, their eyes on him—him alone. He was sure of it. They were astonished. It showed in their expressions. Was that Pete Holman up there with the football team? Really? No kidding? Not Pete Holman, who cut classes, who smoked cigarettes outside the boiler room, who beat up Alan Hollis, who had those other fights. Pete was sure that was what they were saying.

As Pete looked back at the crowd of faces, he remembered his old standard response: Pick one of the faces, set the jaw, narrow the eyes, and stare back, unblinking. It scared people. But this time it was Pete who was scared. He was going to play tonight. Those students out there in the audience—so curious, so puzzled—were going to be in the bleachers, watching. Was Pete Holman, tough guy, able to play football?

When the cheerleaders ran off the stage, Coach Wilson walked on and headed for the lectern. The noise level went up several notches. The coach was smiling and waving. As he watched Coach Wilson, Pete realized that the man had once stood on this stage as a player, just as Pete was doing now.

The coach finally waved the crowd into silence

and began talking. He said the Bulldogs had worked hard and were ready for their game with the Windham Bobcats. That touched off more howling, and Coach Wilson stepped back, waiting.

When the shouting died down, Coach Wilson introduced the Bulldogs' captains—Art Tracy and the middle linebacker, Leon Quick—setting off another round of cheering.

As Pete watched Art and Leon take a step forward, give a little wave, then step back, he couldn't help wondering what the reaction would be if he were introduced—"a new member of the team, Pete Holman." Dead silence, probably, instead of cheers, Pete figured.

Then Coach Wilson said he was sure the Bulldogs would give everything they had—or something like that. He did not predict victory, and Pete remembered that he had heard somewhere that football coaches never did.

Then it was over.

Pete stopped by his locker and picked up the playbook on his way out of the school. He figured it might be a good idea to look over the plays at home before he returned to dress for the game. He could give the plays a quick review while having a snack— no more than that, Coach Wilson had said. A player didn't want to enter a game feeling overstuffed.

In the crowd of students pouring out of the school, Pete heard someone say, "Good luck tonight." It was a moment before he realized the speaker was addressing him. He turned and looked into a face he didn't know. Then he smiled and said, "Thanks."

A block from home, he saw his mother's car in the driveway. Was she ill? Or was something else wrong? Her nights off were Tuesday and Wednesday, not Friday.

Pete quickened his steps. His father's death—so sudden, so unexpected—had impressed on Pete how quickly tragedy could occur. He cut across the front yard to the porch and went inside.

His mother was just walking out of the hall that led to the bedrooms. "You're home," she announced with a smile.

"Is anything wrong?"

"No. I swapped with Elaine. She's working for me tonight and I'll work for her Tuesday night."

"Oh?"

"You're playing a game tonight, aren't you?"

"Yeah."

"You didn't think I'd miss watching my son carry the ball for good ol' Cartwright High, did you?"

"Well, I—" Pete almost blushed. The thought had never entered his mind that his mother might want to watch him play football. As a matter of fact, this was probably the first thing he'd ever done that he didn't mind having his mother watch.

"It's all right, isn't it?"

"Well, sure."

Chapter Ten

The kickoff was minutes away.

Pete, wearing the game uniform of royal blue with large white numerals—22—on his chest and back, stood at the sideline, his helmet dangling from his right hand. He watched the Bulldogs' cocaptains, Art and Leon, walk onto the field for the flip of the coin.

From across the field, the Windham High cocaptains, wearing white uniforms trimmed with red, were approaching.

The scene seemed to glisten in the glare of the arc lights bathing the field.

Pete stared beyond the captains in the center of the field at the bleacher across the way. Then he turned and looked at the one behind the Cartwright High bench. The bleachers on both sides were jammed with people, and most of the crowd was shouting. A lot of them were wearing the blue and white of Cartwright High. But there were also a lot of Windham High fans wearing red and white.

To the left of the bench and behind it, on the cinder track, a pep band was playing.

For Pete, the entire experience was new—from the moment his mother had dropped him off for his six o'clock showup in the locker room to this scene, with all its light, color, and noise.

When he had arrived in the locker room, the place was deathly quiet. What had he expected? He didn't know. So he had quietly gone about changing into his game uniform. When he finished, he noticed that nobody was leaving the room, so he sat on a bench and waited to see what happened next.

Coach Wilson walked by and said, "Ready, Pete?"

"Ready." Pete wasn't all that sure he was ready. He was hoping he didn't fumble the ball or slip and fall or... But he managed to speak the word firmly.

The coach said, "Good," and walked on, moving among the players, asking a question here, patting a shoulder there.

Then Coach Wilson stepped into the middle of the floor, and all faces turned toward him.

"Remember what you've learned," he said. "You've worked hard, and you're ready. Play your best, and winning will take care of itself." He paused and then said, "Let's go."

◆　◆　◆　◆　◆

The referee flipped a coin into the air, somebody called heads or tails, and the referee bent over and squinted at the coin.

The bleachers were strangely silent all of a sudden.

Then the referee signaled that Cartwright High had won the toss, had chosen to receive the opening kickoff, and would defend the north goal.

The bleachers erupted in a giant cheer.

Art and Leon turned and ran back to the sideline, and the players crowded in around them, shouting. Pete joined in the melee.

Then, as quickly as all the jumping and shouting had started, it ended. The kickoff team ran onto the field, and the other players, Pete among them, spread out along the sideline.

Corey Jackson fielded the game's opening kickoff on the eighteen-yard line and raced straight up the middle of the field, battling his way to the thirty-seven-yard line. His first return of the season was a good one. Grinning broadly, he came running off the field. The Cartwright High fans were on their feet, cheering. The players standing along the sideline shouted and reached out to clap Corey on the shoulder pads.

On the first play from scrimmage, Jeff Robbins

battered his way through the middle of the line for six yards. Then Art kept the ball on an option play around right end for four yards and a first down on the forty-seven-yard line.

The Bulldogs seemed to be on the march.

But then Jeff hit a wall of Windham High defenders off right tackle and went down for no gain. Art tried, and missed, a pass into the flat. On third down and ten, Art pitched out wide to Jeff going around left end. Jeff ran the prescribed path, got a good block from Bud Perry, and then went down in the arms of a linebacker. He was three yards short of a first down.

The Bulldogs punted the ball away, and their defensive unit took the field.

Art arrived at the sideline and headed straight for Coach Wilson. The quarterback and the coach were going to discuss what they had learned in the Bulldogs' first possession. The other players in the offensive unit, some of them acknowledging compliments and shouts of encouragement, took up positions along the sideline.

Pete glanced at Jeff. With his helmet unstrapped and tilted back on his head, he was nodding and smiling to someone chattering at him. Maybe Jeff had reason to be pleased. He had gained thirteen yards on three carries. That was not bad. Jeff had run the plays as drawn, as they were practiced. Twice he'd made nice gains. Once he'd been stopped cold.

It was that one time when Jeff was stopped that now flickered through Pete's mind as he watched him on the sideline. The play called for Jeff to run off right tackle, and he had done just that, colliding at the line of scrimmage with two Windham High tacklers who wrapped him up and threw him to the ground.

Why hadn't Jeff cut to the left or the right and taken another route when he saw those Windham High players looming up in front of him? The point of the game was to gain yardage and cross the goal, wasn't it? If running the play as drawn will accomplish that, fine. But if not, why not run somewhere else—to gain yardage?

Jeff had more than two years of experience carrying the ball for the Bulldogs. Pete's total experience in high school football amounted to two weeks of practice. Maybe Jeff knew what he was doing. For sure, Coach Wilson never told Jeff to run away from trouble instead of straight into it. But at the same time, the coach never told Pete to stick to the prescribed route if he thought he could make yardage going another way.

Pete gave a little shrug and turned his attention to the action on the field.

◆　◆　◆　◆　◆

"Holman!"

Pete turned and saw Coach Wilson waving him onto the field.

It was two minutes into the second quarter, and the game was still scoreless. The Bulldogs stood at their own forty-five-yard line with a first down, thanks to a five-yard gain by Art on a keeper around right end.

Pete nodded, pulled on his helmet, and ran onto the field. He checked in with the referee and passed Jeff jogging off the field. They nodded to each other.

Heading toward the huddle, he glanced at the bleachers. Somewhere up there was his mother, probably telling the person seated next to her, "That's my son going into the game." And possibly somewhere up there were Bucky and Jimbo, laughing and telling each other, "Look, ol' Petey's in the game." Or, more likely, Bucky and Jimbo were under the bleachers, oblivious to Pete's entry, nursing a beer or a half-pint of vodka. A year ago that was where Pete had been, too.

Surprisingly, one more face flashed through Pete's mind—Officer Stowell's. Pete wondered what the police officer was thinking about him now.

When Pete took his place in the huddle, leaning forward slightly, hands on knees, he felt his heart pounding and knew his palms were sweaty. He took a deep breath, which didn't help much. Pete Holman nervous? It was a strange new feeling. Pete Holman either handled things or they didn't matter. Nothing was worth getting nervous about. But he couldn't make his heart quit pounding hard.

Art was leaning into the huddle and saying something. Then he was looking at Pete. "You with us?"

Pete nodded jerkily, bringing his mind back to the playing field. "Yeah," he said huskily. His throat was dry.

Art called the play—the same running back plunge off right tackle that had left Jeff piled up on the ground at the line of scrimmage for no gain.

Pete gave a curt nod.

The Bulldogs broke the huddle and lined up. Pete, behind Art, wiped his sweaty palms on his jersey and bent into position.

Art took the snap and, backing up and turning, handed the ball off to Pete.

Pete took the ball and headed for the back of Bryan Warren, the right tackle. Bryan's assignment was to turn the Windham High defender to the inside, freeing Pete to break through and cut to the outside. A lot depended on the Windham High defensive end's overrunning his position, allowing Pete to dash past him. When Jeff had run the play, Bryan lost his battle and Jeff had not been quick

enough to get past the charging defensive end. Both
the tackle and the end had hit him.

Plunging forward, Pete saw the defensive end
slam on the brakes and turn. The end almost—but
not quite—overran Pete. He threw out an arm that
knocked Pete off balance. Pete whirled to get away.
He managed to keep his feet. Then, as the defensive
end fell away, Pete ran toward the right side of
Bryan's back. Bryan was having a tough time turning the defender. The Windham High tackle was
now paying less attention to Bryan's block than
to Pete. It was the ballcarrier he wanted. The defender made a lunge past Bryan.

Pete skipped one step to his right. When he felt
a hand go down his left arm, he pulled his arm up
before the reacher could take hold. Bryan fell in
front of the defender. Whether intentional or not,
Bryan's tumble amounted to the block Pete needed.
One tackler was out of the play.

For a moment Pete seemed free, running to the
outside.

Down the field, he could see emptiness along the
sideline. He ran for it. From somewhere far, far away,
he heard the roar of the fans cheering as they leaped
to their feet.

Then something as hard as iron slammed into his
left hip. He took one more step, trying to spin to get
away. But there was no escape. He was off balance,

with one leg in the grasp of the tackler, and he fell.

Pete leaped to his feet and looked around. A nine-yard gain.

Bud Perry was suddenly in front of Pete. "I'm sorry."

"Sorry?"

"I almost got that linebacker. You would have gone all the way."

From his left tackle position, Bud had raced all the way across the field to try to make a block.

Pete grinned at Bud. "Next time," he said.

Art gained two yards on a quarterback sneak, giving the Bulldogs a first down on the Windham High forty-four-yard line.

A short pass over center failed when Tucker Williamson let the ball zip through his hands. Then Art, with Pete blocking, gained five yards on a roll-out around right end.

It was third down and five to go on the Windham High thirty-nine-yard line.

Art called for Pete to carry the ball up the middle. The Bulldogs' center, Harry Walker, and the two guards had been doing a good job of controlling the middle of the line.

Pete, lining up directly behind Art, charged forward at the moment of the snap and took the ball a couple of yards behind the line of scrimmage. White jerseys with red trim were everywhere in front of him. It looked as if the Windham High Bobcats had known what was coming and had bunched their whole defense in the middle.

Pete cut sharply to his left, almost bumped into the surprised Art, and took two steps parallel to the line of scrimmage. Then he stopped. What now? Not much time to decide.

Bud Perry, at left tackle, was knocking one defender to the ground and going after another. The Windham High middle linebacker had blitzed the center of the line and was out of the play. Now Bud was zeroing in on the linebacker on his side of the line.

Pete spurted into the hole opened by Bud.

He did a little jig in place, giving Bud time to move over in front of him and block out the linebacker. Somebody grabbed for Pete, and he spun, pulling loose, just as Bud cut down the linebacker. Pete sprinted straight ahead, then angled toward the sideline when he spotted a defensive back in pursuit.

The defensive back made a frantic, diving effort to tackle Pete from behind. Pete felt a hand slap him on the hip, and then trail off as he crossed the goal.

Pete tossed the ball to the official coming into the end zone behind him and turned upfield, looking for Bud Perry. Somebody had a hand out and Pete slapped it, then kept jogging toward the spot where Bud had gone down.

He was only vaguely aware of the roaring noise rolling down onto the field from the bleachers on both sides of him. The arc lights seemed even brighter, but the scene in front of him up the field was a hazy, blurred image of players in blue and players in white.

Bud was getting to his feet as Pete ran up to him. Pete clapped him on the back and shouted, "Yeah!" Bud grinned and nodded, draping an arm over Pete's shoulder.

Then they broke and ran toward the sideline.

Art came up alongside Pete. "Beautiful running."

Pete grinned at him.

At the bench, the players mobbed Pete, slapping his helmet, shoulder pads, back—anything they could reach.

Pete got his helmet off, took a deep breath, and decided that he had never felt so good about anything in his entire life.

Chapter Eleven

At halftime the players jogged off the field with the score remaining 7–0.

Pete, sharing the running back position with Jeff Robbins, had carried the ball three more times after the touchdown. His best effort was a fourteen-yard gain up the middle when he spurted between two linemen and spun away from a linebacker's off-balance stab at grabbing him. Suddenly free, Pete thought he was loose for another touchdown until a defensive back pinned his legs together in a diving tackle. On his other two runs, he gained five yards off tackle and was stopped for no gain around end.

Whether he was running and spinning and dodging his way thirty-nine yards to a touchdown or going to the ground for no gain around end, Pete had felt an excitement—his and the crowd's—every time he took the ball in his hands and ran. He heard the roar of the fans and felt a thrill when he darted through a narrow opening and ran for a big gain. He had the same feeling, an almost electric sensation, when he ran for freedom and jumped and spun, only to go down in the arms of a tackler.

As Pete jogged off the field, he spotted Jeff ahead of him and had to admit that he was running well, too. Jeff was making steady gains of four to six yards—not bad, but no long runs, no touchdowns. And, Pete ruefully remembered, no false starts like Pete's lapse on the end run that ended with no gain. He'd almost started the wrong way and, by the time he'd corrected his error, he found himself out of position and came close to bobbling the pitchout. Well, at least he hadn't gone down for a loss.

Approaching the school building, the players narrowed into single file to pass through the doorway and troop into the locker room. They were sweaty, dirt-streaked, breathing hard—and silent.

In the locker room, the scene was neither jubilant nor grim. Pete had figured it might have been jubilant, or at least upbeat. After all, the Bulldogs were in the lead. Or it might have been grim; one touchdown was a slim margin. But more than anything else, the mood was simply businesslike.

Pete looked around the room. What now? He'd never been in a locker room during halftime of a football game. Nor had he even wondered what might happen there.

Was Coach Wilson going to shout and wave his arms a lot? So far, the coach wasn't doing anything, just standing and watching the players as they settled onto benches. He seemed pretty calm. Maybe that was because the Bulldogs were leading. No, Pete decided on second thought, that wasn't it. He figured that Coach Wilson probably was always calm at halftime, no matter what the score was. Pete couldn't imagine Coach Wilson shouting and pleading and waving his arms.

Pete suddenly realized he felt very alone, even in the crowded locker room. Most of the players were sitting or standing around in pairs or small groups— close friends hanging out together. But Pete was alone. He knew the players now—their faces, their names, their positions—but he wasn't a close friend of any of them. He liked some of the players, especially Art. He'd thought at first that the quarterback was just acting like a know-it-all. But gradually he realized that Art was really trying to help him. Still, neither Art nor Bud Perry nor Tucker Williamson— none of them—was a close friend.

No, the guys Pete was used to hanging around with were not here in the locker room. They probably were outside, under the bleacher, taking swigs.

Pete dropped onto a bench and wished the half-time intermission was over. He'd come to feel comfortable with the players on the practice field, especially after his first long run from scrimmage left them all wide-eyed. He had come to feel himself one of them, all of them running and sweating and bumping. And earlier tonight, in his first game under the arc lights, he had felt comfortable with his team- mates as he stood on the sideline or lined up in the backfield. He was one of the team, wearing the same blue uniform with white trim, and all of them had the same goal of defeating the Windham High Bobcats. But sitting in the quiet locker room at half- time, he felt alone and uncomfortable.

His eyes happened to meet those of Alan Hollis. He looked away but not quickly enough. No matter that Pete had run for the game's only touchdown. Alan's stare was unfriendly, almost angry. Clearly, he did not think Pete belonged in a blue and white uniform, running the ball and sitting in the locker room at halftime. And Pete, his eyes now focused on the floor in front of him, thought for the first time that he was to blame for Alan's unfriendly gaze.

Pete watched Coach Wilson walk across and speak with Art. He was surprised when the quarter- back, listening to the coach, turned suddenly and looked at Pete. Had the coach said something to Art about Pete? Then Coach Wilson turned and spoke briefly with Jeff Robbins, who nodded in response.

From there, the coach walked across and began talking to Leon Quick, the middle linebacker. Coach Barnett joined them. The two coaches were

explaining something, and Leon, frowning, was nodding his understanding.

When Coach Wilson moved away from Leon
and Coach Barnett, he turned and walked toward
Pete. Without thinking, Pete got to his feet. Maybe
the coach was going to compliment him on his
touchdown run. At the time, in the midst of the
action of the first half, he had given Pete only a small
smile and a brief nod. Or maybe the coach was
going to comment on Pete's false start on the end
run—a mental error, the kind Jeff Robbins never
made.

The coach was smiling as he approached. "Pete,"
he said without preamble, "you'll be starting the
second half."

Pete blinked in surprise and said nothing. He had
assumed all along that Jeff—more experienced, just
as strong, just about as fast—was the regular running
back, and he was a substitute. Sure, he'd run thirty-
nine yards for the game's only touchdown. And, yes,
he'd had a couple of other pretty good runs. But
he'd made a mistake on the end run. Didn't that
matter? The coach was still smiling. Finally, Pete
nodded to Coach Wilson and said, "Okay."

"No more false starts, right?"

Pete smiled weakly and said, "Right."

Then, almost as an afterthought, the coach said,

"You had some nice runs in the first half. The touchdown run was a beauty. Keep going."

"Sure."

Coach Wilson stepped to the center of the floor and waited for the chatter among the players to fade out.

Pete sat back down. So now he knew that one false start didn't erase the good runs. The coach wanted the good runs without any false starts. Pete understood the message.

Pete turned slightly and glanced at Jeff, who was watching him. Had Jeff been surprised by Coach Wilson's announcement? Maybe not, following Pete's touchdown run. Now Jeff made no sign at all—no smile for Pete, for sure, but also no frown. Jeff just stared at him.

Pete turned his attention back to Coach Wilson, who was speaking.

"You played a good first half, and we're leading by one touchdown." The coach spoke in a normal conversational tone—no shouting, no pleading, no exhorting. His arms hung easily at his sides, and he turned slowly as he spoke, taking in all the players in his gaze.

"But there is another half to go, and the game is a long way from being won. You're going to have to play better in the second half, because the Bobcats have spent this halftime making sure their mistakes won't happen again—and you can bet on it."

The players watched him in silence.

"Okay," Coach Wilson said finally, "let's go."

So, thought Pete, getting to his feet, the Bulldogs have to be better in the second half, and one way to do it is to put Pete Holman in as running back.

Okay!

Chapter Twelve

The Windham High Bobcats took Travis Ward's kickoff opening the second half and marched down the field in nine plays to a touchdown. They kept the ball mostly on the ground, going wide around the ends. They were trying to avoid meeting Leon Quick, looming large at his middle linebacker post. When the Bobcats passed, the throws were short little tosses into the flat, again trying to avoid Leon. After the final play in the drive—a pitchout wide to the left with the runner dashing eight yards to the corner of the end zone—the kick for the extra point tied the score at 7–7.

Pete, watching from the sideline, figured that Coach Wilson had been right. The Bobcats must have corrected their errors during halftime. They must be doing a lot of different things on offense, although the only change Pete recognized was that most of the plays were going out wide, away from Leon.

When Corey Jackson ran onto the field to receive the kickoff, Pete pulled on his helmet, snapped the strap, and stood watching, clenching and unclenching his fists.

Down the sideline, the defensive players were already gathering around Coach Barnett, watching him sketch on chalkboard the changes designed to keep the Bobcats from repeating their touchdown drive.

Corey returned the kickoff twelve yards, to the Cartwright High twenty-nine-yard line, and Pete and the other members of the offensive unit jogged onto the field.

When Pete lined up for the first play, he noticed the Windham High players watching him, especially the middle linebacker. At first he was puzzled. Then he knew what it was. When he'd entered the game in the first half, he'd been a substitute, a name and a number that nobody knew, a second-stringer giving the starter a breather. But now he was a running back who could, they knew, break loose and run through the entire team to the end zone. The realization gave Pete a good feeling. He, Pete Holman, was somebody they had to stop if they hoped to win. He had been a subject of discussion in the Windham High locker room at halftime. Not bad, he thought, for a substitute running back with only two weeks of practice behind him. But the realization also was scary. Could he do it again, now that he was no longer a surprise?

Pete had no more time to wonder. Art was turning, extending the ball to him.

Pete ran past Art, taking in the ball, and threw himself toward the center of the line. He spotted a crack between the center, Harry Walker, and the right guard and veered toward it. He was going through when the linebacker slammed into him. Pete whirled furiously, trying to pull himself free. The linebacker held on. Pete gave a final lunge and fell to the ground.

He had gained an extra yard, maybe a little more, with the last surge in the grasp of the linebacker— a total gain of five yards, to the Cartwright High thirty-four-yard line.

Getting to his feet, Pete glanced at the linebacker. No doubt about it, he had been watching Pete—and waiting for him.

Art then picked away at the Windham High defense with every weapon he had—except Pete Holman. Probably Art had recognized the Windham tactic of watching and waiting for Pete, or maybe Coach Wilson had foreseen it and warned Art to be on the alert in the second half. Art rolled out around end. He pitched out to the fullback, Kevin Hughes, and he handed off to Kevin plunging into the middle of the line. He passed to the sideline, into the flat, and over center—without calling Pete's number again.

It finally dawned on Pete that with the Windham defense wary of the threatening newcomer at running back, others in the Cartwright High attack were gaining a half-step advantage. A fake handoff to Pete froze the Windham High defense.

The strategy, helped by a spectacular sideline catch by Tucker Williamson, moved the Bulldogs through three first downs to the Windham High forty-yard line as the third quarter drew near a close.

In the huddle, Art looked at Pete and said, "Okay—now."

"Huh?"

Art called the play, sending Pete off right tackle, behind Bryan Warren.

Pete nodded.

Art took the snap, stepped back, faked a pitchout to Kevin going left, turned, and handed off the ball to Pete. Pete nestled the ball in his right hand and ran toward Bryan's right shoulder. Bryan was struggling to turn the tackle to the inside, giving Pete a corridor for running. Bryan seemed to be winning the battle.

Then, out of nowhere, the defensive end rose up in front of Pete. Pete cut sharply to his right and ran wide, around the lunging end, away from the opening Bryan was trying to create. He escaped the end and sprinted toward the sideline.

The startling shift in direction left the Windham defenders running the wrong way and brought the spectators to their feet with a loud cheer.

Near the sideline, Pete turned upfield and saw ahead nothing but empty space. He was alone, free of tacklers but also bereft of blockers outside the pattern of the play. No matter. The end would have nailed him if he'd stayed on the proper path. Then the empty space began to fill up with white uniforms. Pete cut back toward the center of the field, weaving through the confusion. He broke one tackle, then another, and finally went down on the Windham High nineteen-yard line—a gain of twenty-one yards.

Art was grinning in the huddle. "Let's try it the other way."

Pete wasn't grinning. His false start on the pitchout play in the first half leaped back into his mind. He mustn't let it happen again. His face wore a mask of determination. He nodded as they broke the huddle.

Then Pete was running. He took in the pitchout going left. He ran wide, looking at what was in front of him. It was not a happy scene. His long run had reawakened in the defense the threat of the new running back. They were watching him from the start of the play. White jerseys were moving out wide with him and now were beginning to close in.

Out of the corner of his eye Pete saw Bud Perry throw his big body in front of a tackler and knock him back. On instinct, Pete cut sharply and darted into the opening. Kevin, angling over in front of Pete, bumped another tackler out of Pete's path. Pete veered to his right, back to the center of the field, then weaved through tacklers to his left.

At the ten-yard line Pete spun away from the grasp of a defensive back. Already off balance, the back fell to the ground, and Pete ran the last steps into the end zone untouched.

He turned in the end zone and tossed the ball to the referee just before Kevin slammed into him with a bear hug. Art was right behind, pounding on Pete's shoulder pads.

As he jogged toward the bench, Pete looked up at the packed bleachers, at everyone standing and shouting.

At the bench, the screaming, jumping players mobbed him.

Finally, he worked his way free, stepped aside, took off his helmet, and watched Travis Ward kick the extra point.

The world, he decided, was a wonderful place.

◆　◆　◆　◆　◆

In the locker room after the game, the mood was no longer businesslike, and Pete Holman no longer felt alone.

The Cartwright High Bulldogs were the winners by a score of 21–7. Art added the Bulldogs' third touchdown on a sixteen-yard rollout around left end. And the Bulldogs' defense stifled the Bobcats.

The locker room was pandemonium—with shouts and laughter and flying towels.

Grinning and laughing, Pete slapped hands and kept saying over and over again, to one player or another, "Thanks." One who slapped hands with him was Jeff Robbins. One who didn't was Alan Hollis.

Finally, the celebration died down, and the players began moving into the showers. Pete was still grinning as he lathered up under the needles of hot water.

When Pete stepped out of the locker room, the first face he saw among the parents and friends of the players waiting in the hallway was Officer Stowell's.

He was in uniform. Maybe he had been the police officer assigned to the game. The police always had an officer somewhere at Cartwright High games to keep troublemakers in line. Pete knew that for a fact.

Officer Stowell was smiling at Pete. He extended his right hand. "Congratulations. Great game."

Pete grinned back. He couldn't quit grinning. He took the officer's hand and shook it. "Thanks."

All around them the hallway was filled with people meeting players and with players getting organized to go off in twos, threes, and fours. Some were going to parties. Others were heading for one of the student hangouts.

From his left side, Pete heard a familiar voice. "You're a hero."

Pete turned to face Jimbo. He was wearing a sloppy grin, and his head tilted a little.

Behind Jimbo, Bucky was grinning and swaying slightly. He echoed Jimbo's statement. "Yeah, a real hero."

Pete looked back at Officer Stowell. The policeman was studying Jimbo. Then he turned away and moved into the crowd, toward the locker room door. He called over his shoulder, "Talk to you later, Pete," and then he was gone.

"Let's go, buddy," Jimbo said. "We've got to celebrate. Two things to celebrate—you're a star and Bucky's got wheels again."

Bucky piped up with a silly grin, "My ol' man let me out of jail today."

Pete looked from Jimbo to Bucky and back to

Jimbo. Pete wasn't grinning now. He didn't want trouble on this, the best night of his life. And that was what Jimbo and Bucky were offering—trouble. Officer Stowell undoubtedly recognized Bucky as the one brought in after the sideswiping two weeks ago and probably figured that Jimbo had been the one who got away. Pete did not want to go with them on this night.

He looked around—for Art, or anyone, who might say, "C'mon with us." Then he could go. But nobody called to him.

"You coming?" Jimbo asked.

"Look," Pete said finally. "Where are you going? My mother brought me, and she's waiting for me over there. I could meet you."

"Where we going?" Bucky sang out.

Jimbo, no longer grinning, watched Pete a moment. Then he said, "Catch up with us at Mickey's." It was a drive-in near the mall. "We'll be waiting for you."

"Right."

Chapter Thirteen

"**D**o you want me to drop you somewhere?" Pete's mother asked in the car.

"No."

"You just want to go home?" A tone of mild surprise was in the question. Pete was always ready to go anyplace but home. Beth Holman knew that.

"Yeah, just home."

She drove a moment without speaking, then said, "It's a big night. I thought—"

Pete looked at his mother. She had seen him talking with Jimbo and Bucky in the hallway outside the locker room. He had seen her watching them. She must have thought they were making plans. Was she suggesting that he ought to meet Jimbo and Bucky? No, probably she figured the players would be gathering to celebrate their victory and that Pete would want to be with them. But none of the players had invited him to join them. Only Jimbo and Bucky, and he didn't want to be with them. Finally, he said, "I'm tired. Long night, you know."

"Yes, it was."

Pete slouched back in the seat for the rest of the ride home, experiencing an unusual feeling of satisfaction that he was making the right move.

His mother was sitting at the redwood table on the deck with a cup of coffee, reading the newspaper, when Pete got up the next morning. He pulled on a pair of gym shorts and a sweatshirt, poured himself a glass of orange juice, and walked out to join her.

"I'm not sure you're ready for this," she said with a smile.

"What?"

She lifted out the sports section of the Cartwright *Morning Herald* and laid it in front of him.

Pete looked down at a picture of himself, the white numerals—22—clearly visible, even his face recognizable. He was carrying the ball tucked in his right arm. His left hand was extended, shoving away a tackler. Pete sat down and stared at the picture.

The headline beneath the picture read: HOLMAN LEADS BULLDOGS TO VICTORY.

Pete had never seen his name printed in such large letters. And never in the Cartwright *Morning Herald* at all.

Pete read the first paragraph: "The Cartwright High Bulldogs unveiled a new running sensation,

Pete Holman, and defeated the Windham High Bobcats 21–7 last night in the season's first game for both teams."

And the second paragraph: "Holman, a substitute running back playing in his first game, came off the bench and ran for two touchdowns and 129 yards."

A few paragraphs down the writer called Pete "a spectacular runner" and said his performance was "sensational." Pete was, the writer said, "a powerful new weapon, totally unexpected, in the Cartwright High arsenal." With Pete Holman, the writer said, "the Bulldogs have to be counted as a premier contender for the Northwest Suburban Conference championship."

Pete looked up. "Well," he said, and smiled.

"Mr. Touchdown," his mother said.

Pete nodded. Then he had a funny thought. It was two weeks ago tonight that he had been sitting in the police station, and Coach Wilson had signed him out on the condition that he join the football team. Two weeks. It seemed a lot longer!

At midmorning Coach Wilson called. "You've seen the *Morning Herald*?"

"Yes."

The coach gave a little chuckle. "Don't believe everything you read."

"Okay."

"You did have an outstanding game."

"Thank you."

The line was silent a moment, and Pete wondered why the coach was calling. Surely it wasn't just to tell him not to get a big head. Or just to compliment him.

"You're going to stick it out, aren't you?"

The question surprised Pete. "Stick it out," he repeated.

"I've thought every day, from the start, that you might just shrug and walk away. Now I want to know if you're on the team to stay."

On the team to stay? The coach's question—for it was a question—caught Pete off balance. Sure, he had come close to walking away from all the sweat and sore muscles and strange looks from teammates. But that was a lot of days ago. Was his performance in last night's game the performance of a player on the brink of quitting, just walking away? Then Pete recalled that Officer Stowell had seen him with Jimbo and Bucky outside the locker room. The policeman must have told Coach Wilson about that. And the coach had no way of knowing what Pete would do, so now he was asking.

"I'm on the team to stay," Pete said.

Through the weekend, wherever Pete went, people waved and called out to him. They shouted his name and said, "Great game!" Everyone in Cartwright seemed to know him. A stranger waved from a car while Pete was cutting grass. The checkout woman at the supermarket somehow knew Pete when he bought a carton of ice cream. A small boy passing by on a bicycle, a total stranger, surprised Pete by saying, "Hi, Pete," as if they had known each other for years.

Pete smiled back at a world he had never known existed.

Neither Jimbo nor Bucky telephoned on Saturday or Sunday.

At school on Monday morning, Pete barely had a chance to take in the new banner on the wall in the lobby—BEAT MEADOWCLIFF—before he was surrounded by students, some of them football players. Pete felt as if he were standing in a spotlight. And he liked it.

While he was walking toward his first class, Art fell in step with him. "I don't know if Coach Wilson mentioned it, but you should always bring your playbook to practice on Monday."

"Oh?"

"Yeah, Coach Wilson always has at least one new play for the upcoming opponent and sometimes a few new wrinkles in some of the old plays. You know, a little surprise or two."

"Uh-huh. I see."

"Have you got yours with you?"

Luckily, Pete had scooped up the playbook with his other books when he'd left home for school. "Yeah, it's in my locker."

At lunch, Pete came out of the cafeteria line with Leon Quick and Bryan Warren. Leon and Bryan headed for a table crowded with football players—and Pete moved along behind them, carrying his tray.

Halfway to the table he saw Jimbo, Bucky, and Rusty seated at their usual table on the other side of the cafeteria. Jimbo was watching him. Then Jimbo said something, and Bucky and Rusty turned and looked.

For a moment, Pete had the urge to turn and walk across to their table. Maybe he owed them an explanation for not showing up at Mickey's on Friday night. He could always tell them he was just too tired to go rambling with them. That wouldn't explain the rest of the weekend, but it would give them a reason for his failure to show up after saying he would meet them. But then Leon turned his head toward Pete and said, "Coming?"

"Yeah," Pete said.

Jimbo, Bucky, and Rusty were still watching when he put his tray on the table and sat down.

◆ ◆ ◆ ◆ ◆

When everyone was dressed for practice, Coach Barnett took the defensive players out to begin warm-up calisthenics, and Coach Wilson passed out two pages for the offensive players' playbooks.

Pete, seated on a bench, looked at the two new plays. Then he looked across at Coach Wilson. He understood now why the coach had called and asked, "Are you going to stick it out?" Both of the new plays featured the running back—Pete—in new ways. Pete knew that if he had sounded shaky or uncertain on the telephone with Coach Wilson, these would not have been this week's new plays.

"Any questions?" Coach Wilson asked.

Nobody spoke. Most of the players were inserting the pages into their playbooks.

"Look them over tonight, and we'll start work on them tomorrow. As you can see, the object is to get Holman loose in an open field with the football in his hands."

Pete avoided the eyes that were on him. He watched the coach. Then he bent and concentrated on his playbook.

Bucky seemed to be waiting for Pete on Tuesday when he came out of his American history class and turned toward the cafeteria. But before either Bucky or Pete could speak, Jimbo's voice came from behind Pete. "What are you doing hanging around with this jock?"

Pete turned. Jimbo was scowling—maybe at Pete, maybe at Bucky.

"Aw, c'mon, Jimbo," Bucky said.

"What's your problem?" Pete said.

Jimbo turned to Pete. "It's not my problem. I've got no problem. You're the one with the problem."

Bucky took a short step forward. "Cut it out, Jimbo."

Jimbo turned on Bucky. "Don't you know that Mr. Big Shot doesn't have any time for us? He's too good for us." Then Jimbo turned to stare at Pete, seeming to dare him to speak.

Pete stared back a moment, then said, "Jimbo, for crying out loud…"

Jimbo put on his best sneer. "You make me sick. Our good buddy. Old friend. Until, that is, the football jocks start liking you. And then—*poof*—there you go. 'So long, old buddies, I just made a better deal. I'm a big guy now—and you're not.' "

Some of the students passing by in the hallway were turning to watch and listen as they went.

"Jimbo…" Bucky's voice was almost a plea.

"Are you too stupid to see what's happening? We're not good enough for ol' Petey now."

"Jimbo," Pete said, trying to keep his voice low.

"You're just a little bit paranoid. Just because I'm on the football team…" Then he let the words trail off. He was going to say that being on the football team didn't make him a different person. But that wasn't true. He *was* a different person. "What I mean is…"

"See," Jimbo said. "C'mon, Bucky, let's go."

Jimbo walked away, and Bucky, with a glance back at Pete, followed.

Chapter Fourteen

By Friday evening, Pete had left the episode with Jimbo and Bucky behind. He'd seen them in classrooms, the hallways, and the cafeteria, but always at a distance. They had made no move to speak and neither had he.

On the practice field that week, the Bulldogs had run—and run, and run again—the two new plays. They were simple plays, nothing fancy. In one, Pete took a shovel pass—a short, underhanded throw—from Art while running wide. Pete found the shovel pass easier to catch than one of Art's whistling bullets. Also, Art could deliver the shovel pass faster than a standard cock-and-throw pass, putting the ball in Pete's hands in a forward position more quickly. In the other new play, Art rolled out and sent a pitchout to Pete coming back the other way. Pete then dived into the line wherever he saw an opening.

The plays had worked well against the Bulldogs' defensive unit. Time and again, Pete had taken in the ball, measured the defense, found an opening, and—leaping to one side or the other, or sweeping out wide, or reversing his field—had run and wriggled and spun and fought his way down the field.

Now, in a matter of hours, he'd be doing it for real—against the Meadowcliff High Tigers.

As he rode in silence with his mother to Cartwright High, where the players would dress and board a bus for the short drive to neighboring Meadowcliff, Pete recalled Coach Wilson's words of caution. This game would be different, the coach had told him. Pete, being new, had surprised Windham High. But he was not going to surprise Meadowcliff. The Tigers were going to be ready for him, lying in wait for him. So it might be pretty tough, the coach had warned.

"Okay?" his mother asked.

"Okay," Pete answered.

Pete changed quickly into his uniform—white with blue numerals and trim for the Bulldogs' role as visiting team—and walked out of the locker room. He went down the corridor and out into the parking lot to the bus. He climbed aboard, looked around, and dropped into a seat next to Bryan Warren.

Bud Perry, passing in the aisle with the stream of players getting on the bus, clapped Pete on a shoulder pad and said, "Get 'em." Bud was big, strong, and good at his position, and he always seemed so confident, so sure of himself. He was showing none of the nervousness that Pete was feeling now.

"Yeah, right," Pete said.

Pete drummed his fingers on the armrest. He knew he was a different Pete Holman from a week ago. Nobody told him "Get 'em" then. Going into the last game he had been a substitute waiting for a chance to play. His highest hope had been to avoid making a dumb play. Now it was different. Now he was supposed to be great.

A week ago, it hadn't mattered. Now it did.

The players were strung out along the sideline. The field was empty in the glare of the arc lights except for the referee awaiting the arrival of the captains for the toss of the coin.

The linemen had finished their pregame bumping and colliding. The backs had moved down the field in their signal drill. Travis Ward had taken his practice kicks at the uprights. Jeff Robbins had punted, and Corey Jackson had caught the punts and then run a few steps forward.

On both sides of the field, the bleachers were packed with people. Many wore the black and gold of the Meadowcliff High Tigers. Others wore the blue and white of Cartwright High.

Pete's mother was up there somewhere. Her

friend Elaine had agreed to another swap.

Looking around, Pete wondered if Officer Stowell was in one bleacher or the other, having come to watch the game—to watch him. Probably not, Pete decided. More likely, the policeman was on duty and bound by the Cartwright city limits.

Pete turned his attention back to the field. Art and Leon were walking out for the toss of the coin. Three players in black with gold trim were approaching from the opposite side.

Unconsciously, Pete wiped a sweaty palm on his jersey.

The going was tough for Pete in the first quarter.

By the time the teams were changing ends of the field for the start of the second quarter, the Bulldogs were out front, 7–0. But it wasn't Pete's running, or the work of the offense, that put them in the lead. Alan Hollis had picked off a wobbly pass and raced thirty-two yards down the sideline for the game's only score.

From the start, there was no doubt that the Meadowcliff High Tigers knew about—and had planned for—the threat of Pete Holman, Cartwright High's new running back.

Time and again, Pete took a handoff from Art, looked for a hole to run through—and found none. His little stutter step on runs into the line, which had given him time to locate cracks in the defense the previous week, produced no openings. When running wide, Pete looked ahead to see defenders moving out to challenge him. And, looking over his shoulder with the idea of cutting sharply toward a promising opening, he saw nothing but black jerseys with gold trim.

Pete carried the ball five times in the first quarter. His best gainer was six yards behind Bud Perry. His total production was eighteen yards. All of the Meadowcliff High defenders were watching Pete, and some of them chased him even when he didn't have the ball.

Now, joining the huddle for the first play of the second quarter, Pete told himself that nobody scores a touchdown every time he carries the ball. Nobody rips off a long gainer every time. But, still, there had to be a way to get through those crowds of defenders wearing black jerseys.

"It's called keying," Art said to Pete with a small smile. Art seldom smiled, either in practice or in games. But he was giving Pete a reassuring smile now.

"Huh?" Pete said. Was Art reading his mind? Yes, probably Pete's frustration showed on his face.

"They're keying on you, same as Windham did in the second half," Art said. "Hang in there. We'll make something happen."

Pete nodded.

Coach Wilson had not yet had the Bulldogs run either of the new plays. He had explained that he wanted to spring the surprises when the Bulldogs were within striking distance of the goal. But so far they had found themselves in a terrible field position each time they took up the attack. The cautious Tigers kept backing up the Bulldogs with punts and then playing tenacious defense.

As if giving Pete a vote of confidence, Art called a play sending Pete inside left tackle, behind Bud Perry.

The Bulldogs broke the huddle and lined up at the Cartwright High thirty-three-yard line, second down and eight yards to go for a first down.

Pete stared across at a middle linebacker who was watching him. He heard Art calling the signals. Then Art was turning and extending the ball.

Pete leaped forward, took in the ball, and angled toward Bud's broad shoulders. Bud was moving his opponent to the left, creating a sliver of space. Pete ran for the opening. He bumped into Bud, then bounced off and kept going. A lineman got a hand on his shoulder. Pete twisted furiously, trying to pull away. The lineman was falling, losing his grip, when the middle linebacker slammed into Pete just above the knees, knocking him to the ground.

Pete got to his feet and looked around—a two-yard gain. He shook his head and walked back to the huddle.

On the next play, Art missed Tucker Williamson on a pass to the left sideline, and Jeff came in to punt.

The Tigers' punt returner, a tiny flea of a guy, and just as quick as one, skittered all over the field and came within a step of going all the way to the goal. Bryan finally caught him and slammed him to the ground on the Bulldogs' twenty-nine-yard line.

The Tigers were beginning the possession with their deepest penetration of the game.

As the Bulldogs' defensive unit trotted onto the field, Pete stood at the sideline, helmet in his hand, and stared across the field. He turned and looked down the line of players at Coach Wilson, now standing bent over with hands on thighs, peering at the scene in front of him. Pete's line of sight landed on Jeff, standing with Art. Both were watching the players on the field. Probably Jeff was wondering if Coach Wilson, disappointed with Pete's showing, would send him into the game. Jeff had been the starter last week. He wasn't the starter this week. Was Pete letting him win his way back? Pete frowned, a little surprised at how much the thought disturbed him.

On the field, the Tigers punched through the

line in three plays to a first down on the Bulldogs' eighteen-yard line. Then an end sweep gained seven yards to the eleven-yard line. From there, the quarterback lofted a pass into a corner of the end zone, barely beyond the leaping reach of Alan Hollis and into the hands of the wide receiver.

With the kick, the score was tied at 7–7.

The Bulldogs took up the attack at their own thirty-one-yard line after Corey Jackson's runback of the kickoff.

Art rolled out to his left and gained five yards when Bud Perry leveled two tacklers with a mighty lunge. Kevin got four yards off right tackle, and Art sneaked behind Harry Walker for two yards and a first down on the forty-two-yard line.

Art was avoiding Pete. With the defense zeroing in on Pete, the other ballcarriers picked up an advantage.

Kevin hit the middle for no gain and then ran wide for four yards before being knocked out of bounds. Art's pass to Tucker gained five yards—one short of a first down—and the Bulldogs punted the ball away again.

For the remainder of the half the two teams rocked back and forth. Pete, in his only carry in the second quarter, gained eight yards when he ran off tackle and reversed his field, weaving through a crowd of tacklers. For an instant, he thought he was free. But then a swarm of Meadowcliff defenders surrounded and buried him.

Pete sat on a bench in the locker room and watched Coach Wilson. The coach was talking to Art, and Art was nodding his understanding. Then the coach walked across to Kevin and Jeff and said something. Pete couldn't tell which of them he was talking to. Coach Wilson moved on to join Coach Barnett and Leon Quick and others on the defense. Then he looked around, spotted Pete, and walked toward him.

Bud Perry leaned over toward Pete and said, "Don't worry, partner, we'll spring you loose in the second half."

Pete looked up, gave a slight smile, and said, "Okay."

Coach Wilson was still coming, and Pete felt a sense of dread as he got to his feet. Had the coach told Art that Jeff was starting the second half, and then told Jeff? Was he now coming to tell Pete? Was this a replay of last Friday night, but in reverse?

Coach Wilson smiled as he stepped in front of Pete. "They're ganging up on you, but don't worry. It'll be different in the second half. Keep punching."

Pete nodded and waited for the coach to continue.

But Coach Wilson said nothing more, turning and walking toward the center of the room.

The third quarter was six minutes old. The Bulldogs stood at their own forty-four-yard line. It was third down and three yards to go for a first down. They had recovered a fumble to stop the Tigers' first drive of the second half.

In just two plays—a line plunge and then an end run by Kevin—Pete sensed a change in the Meadowcliff defenders. Before, they had kept wary, alert eyes on Pete with every snap of the ball. On every play, they seemed to be waiting for Pete—just him—whether he had the ball or not. But now something had changed. The defenders felt they had beaten him. They were less worried, less wary. Their confidence showed in their eyes. And in their movements, too—almost relaxed when they tracked the empty-handed Pete Holman.

"Let me have it," Pete said to Art in the huddle. "They're barely watching me now."

Art looked at Pete a moment. Maybe Art had also sensed the change. He called a quick opener, with Pete carrying up the middle.

Pete took the handoff and threw himself at the center of the line. He bounced off Harry Walker and a guard struggling with an onrushing lineman, whirled, and ran to his left. Just outside end, he stopped, looked, and cut back between end and tackle. He caught the defenders leaning the wrong way and bumped his way through to the secondary. The middle linebacker was coming across to meet him—and then disappeared, cut down by Kevin.

Pete swerved to his left, again running for the outside, away from the crowd of tacklers now in pursuit.

He was loose in the open field, aiming for the sideline, when a defensive back caught one ankle with a diving tackle and he went down on the Meadowcliff High thirty-five-yard line—a gain of twenty-one yards.

By the time Pete was getting to his feet, Coach Wilson was speaking to a substitute guard at the sideline and sending him into the game.

To Pete's surprise, the guard's message in the huddle was to send Pete out wide in one of the new plays. Surely the defenders were going to be back on the alert, not relaxed, and they were going to be wary, not overconfident about Pete Holman.

"Good," was all Art said. He looked at Pete. "If it works, it'll break their backs." He looked around the huddle. "We've got to make it work."

Pete nodded.

Art took the snap. Pete turned and ran to his left. Art stepped back quickly, holding the ball low while

Kevin came by going to his right. He extended the ball to Kevin, then pulled it back, turned, and shoveled an underhanded pass to Pete. Pete, looking back, reached out and took in the ball waist high without breaking stride.

Pete was a step outside Bud Perry. Bud let his opponent burst into the backfield to find nothing but Art without the ball. Then Bud charged into the secondary, looking for somebody to knock down.

Pete slammed on the brakes, turned, and followed Bud.

A linebacker, recovering quickly, came across. Pete did a little dance in place, giving Bud time to cross in front of him and crash into the linebacker.

A defensive back was coming up fast, fighting his way around the tangle of arms and legs Bud had created.

Pete went the other way.

The defensive back reached out and grabbed Pete's right arm—his ball-carrying arm—and hung on. Pete felt the ball wobble. He clapped his left hand over the ball and, with both hands on it, spun furiously. He pulled the clinging defensive back off his feet and flung him away.

Coming out of the spin, Pete looked around frantically. Which way to run? The ducking, pulling, and spinning had upset the compass in his head.

Then he saw a crowd of black jerseys bearing down on him from his right.

He was wide left. The tacklers were coming from his right. Suddenly his compass clicked back into action. He ran the remaining yards to the goal.

Chapter Fifteen

Travis Ward's kick made the score 14–7—and there it stood until the end of the game.

Neither team mustered a serious threat in the remaining minutes of the third quarter or throughout the fourth quarter. Twice more, Pete broke loose for long gains—one for fifteen yards, one for thirteen yards—but both times the Meadowcliff High defenders stiffened and stopped the Bulldogs from moving on down the field.

The Bulldogs carried the tension of the tight game from the field when they walked toward the bus waiting to return them to Cartwright High. Players who might have been cheering a close victory over a tough opponent seemed more relieved than elated.

Pete was sure he had gained more than a hundred yards rushing. He knew from the few games he'd watched on television that a hundred-yard performance was pretty good, and now he'd done it twice in a row. But as he milled around with the others in the parking lot he felt a sense of frustration. Too many times the Meadowcliff tacklers—"keying" on him, as Art put it—had closed the door on him.

The parking lot was crowded with students, parents, and friends of the players gathered around the bus. The fans were neither as tense nor as weary as the players, and there was a lot of laughter, shouts of congratulation, and an occasional cheer of victory.

Pete was standing alongside the bus again when Art walked up from the side and said, "Some of us are going to pick up a pizza and come over to my house after we've changed. Want to come along?"

"Sure," Pete said, and then realized he wasn't even surprised by the invitation. He added, "I've got to find my mother and tell her not to wait for me at school—there she is."

Pete trotted across to tell his mother. When she seemed about to frown, he thought, No, there's no Jimbo, no Bucky here tonight, and he said, "I'm going over to Art Tracy's house with some of the players."

She smiled at him and nodded. "Good game."

"Thanks."

When he turned to head back to the bus he saw Officer Stowell grinning and giving him a thumbs-up signal. So he *was* here, after all. Pete returned the gesture and joined the line of players shuffling toward the door of the bus.

With everyone aboard, Coach Wilson stood at the front of the bus, waiting a moment until he had everyone's attention.

"You played well tonight, and you deserved to win," he said. "It was a tough game, and those are the best ones to win."

Then he nodded to the driver, and the bus began moving out of the parking lot. As it rolled along the darkened suburban streets on the short run to Cartwright High, Coach Wilson moved down the aisle, leaning in occasionally to make a comment or ask about a bump or a bruise.

To Pete he said, "In a close game, one big play can make the difference between winning and losing. I knew you had it in you to make the big play we needed. And you did it."

Pete mumbled, "Thanks," feeling a little embarrassed, knowing that Tucker Williamson, sitting next to him, had heard the coach's remark. Then Coach Wilson moved on.

It was a couple of moments before Pete translated what the coach had said. The Bulldogs would not have won tonight if it hadn't been for Pete Holman. The jocks—who two weeks ago had had no time for him, nor he for them—would have lost or at best settled for a tie, without Pete Holman.

He remembered feeling so alone in the locker room at halftime a week ago. He did not feel at all alone now.

It wasn't like Friday night out on the town with Jimbo and Bucky. Not at all.

After showering and dressing in the Cartwright High locker room, a dozen or so of the players— Alan Hollis among them, Pete noted with a flicker of concern—piled into cars. They stopped at Bruno's to pick up pizzas. Then they headed for Art's house and settled themselves into the large basement den. They ate the pizzas, washed them down with sodas, and rehashed the game.

Pete heard more from the players about almost running the wrong way on his touchdown run than about the touchdown itself or his impressive rushing yardage statistics. He hadn't known that his moment of disorientation was so obvious.

"I thought for sure you were going to run the wrong way when you got through flip-flopping around with that defensive back," Art said.

Pete looked at the grinning faces and said, "I did, too," and everyone laughed.

Bud said, "You'd have been famous forever at Cartwright High as Wrong-Way Holman."

Pete shrugged. "Missed my chance, I guess."

"Just as well," Bud said. "We would have killed you." Everyone laughed again.

Later, Jeff and Bryan played pool, and Pete stood and watched them for several minutes. Pete had developed into a pretty good pool player at Ernie's Parlor during the summer, occasionally winning a few bucks off men who didn't think a high school boy with a cigarette between his lips could play the game. But he had no desire to revive memories of those days at this table here tonight.

Alan and Tucker were banging away at the Ping-Pong table at the other end of the room. Pete drifted over toward them, watching Alan uncertainly. He and Alan hadn't exchanged a single word since Pete joined the team. With Pete playing offense and Alan defense, it was easy for them to avoid each other.

As Pete approached, Alan was serving. Pete watched as the two volleyed. When Tucker slammed the ball into the net, ending the play, Pete said to Alan, "Your interception and runback—they were great." Then he waited as Alan watched him without speaking. Finally, Alan said, "Thanks," as he grabbed the ball tossed across the net by Tucker. He was serving again as Pete walked away.

Okay, Pete thought, so what? If Alan wants to stay mad, that's his business. I'm on the football team, whether Alan Hollis likes it or not. And I'm here tonight with the players, no matter what Alan thinks.

As he looked around, he remembered other Friday nights and decided that this was really different.

There was no half-pint of vodka being passed around, no beers he and his friends had talked someone into buying for them. Nobody was smoking. Nobody suggested spray painting a wall, and nobody mentioned gunning around town in a car just for the thrill of it.

Different, really different—and better.

As he moved away from the Ping-Pong table, Pete's ears perked up when he heard Officer Stowell's name being mentioned.

Art was doing the talking, saying something about Officer Stowell's being at the game at Meadowcliff High.

Pete stopped to listen, more than a little fearful of what he might hear, even uneasy about looking around to see if any of the players were watching him when Officer Stowell was mentioned. Pete had never told anyone but Bucky and Jimbo about the role that the police officer played in putting him on the football team—and stories told by Bucky and Jimbo probably never made it into this circle. But maybe Officer Stowell or Coach Wilson had told the story.

Pete took a seat at the end of a sofa near Art, who was seated cross-legged on the floor beside a low coffee table. Bud, Kevin, and Bryan were seated in the circle.

Bud said, "He's never missed a game in the three years that I've been playing, no matter whether it's at home or away."

Kevin nodded. "Sometimes he's only there for a little while, like when he's on duty and stops by on his dinner hour. But every game—he's there to see at least a little of it."

"Well, he used to play for Cartwright High," Art said, "but there's more to it than that."

"What do you mean?" Bryan asked.

Pete leaned forward, interested.

"My father went through school with Officer Stowell," Art continued.

"They played together on the Bulldogs?"

"Yeah. My father was the quarterback the year before Coach Wilson, and Stowell played fullback on that year's team—but only one year, his senior year."

"Go on."

"Well, Officer Stowell used to run with a pretty tough crowd. My father says he always knew who Bill Stowell was, but that was about all. He was in and out of trouble all the time. And the summer before his senior year he and some of his buddies swiped a car and went for a joyride. They got caught—with Stowell at the wheel."

There was a moment of silence. Then Bryan said, "Officer Stowell? Swiped a car?"

Pete sat without moving, waiting for Art to continue.

"The man who was the Cartwright police chief back in those days told Stowell that since the car wasn't damaged he'd let him go—but only if he turned out for football practice, which was starting the following week."

"It's hard to imagine Officer Stowell stealing a car," Kevin said.

"Yeah," Bud said. "Always so straight and proper in his uniform."

"Well, it happened, and that's what made a football player out of Bill Stowell. He went out for football to get off the hook with the police chief. My father says he wasn't very fast, but he was strong, and he never quit. He made the all-conference team, and he was offered a football scholarship at Northern Illinois. But he never went there to play. Instead, he attended police school for two years, and then the chief hired him on the force here."

Pete was frowning. So there was more to the story than what Officer Stowell had told him when they were seated on the deck last Saturday. Pete heard in his mind his own words in asking Officer Stowell why he had sent him to the football team:

"Nobody does anything for nothing." The memory made him cringe. A police chief had done something for Bill Stowell for nothing. And Bill Stowell had done something for Pete Holman for nothing.

Pete looked at the players around him. Did any of them know what had put Pete Holman on the football team? They all knew his background, his reputation—same as Art's father had known Bill Stowell's. Had anyone here put two and two together?

Nobody was looking at Pete, and nobody said anything.

It was after eleven o'clock when Bryan dropped Pete off at home.

Pete stood alone at the curb in the darkness a moment. It might have been a night like this when Bill Stowell got caught driving a stolen car—and a kindly police chief sent him off to the football team. And it had been a night like this when Pete Holman got picked up, after Bucky smashed into a parked car.

Maybe someday it would be his turn to repay the debt—do something for somebody for nothing.

Pete walked into the house.

Chapter Sixteen

Following the last class on Monday, Pete headed down the hall toward his locker to drop off some books and pick up his playbook for the weekly addition of one or two new plays.

He walked through the lobby and glanced up at the large white banner with blue lettering: BEAT HANSON HIGH.

"All right!" he said to himself.

Here it was only Monday, and already he was looking forward to the game. That was another big change in his life since joining the football team—he had something to look forward to, something to work toward. Always before, Monday had been just the boring beginning of another nothing week.

Even the weekends were better. There was the game on Friday night, of course. And last Friday night there had been the gathering at Art's house after the game—more fun than looking for trouble with Jimbo and Bucky. There'd be other Friday night parties, he was sure. On Saturday and Sunday there were the waves of greetings around town from acquaintances and strangers alike. They knew who Pete Holman was, and they liked him. It was a good feeling.

When he ran into Officer Stowell in an aisle in Wardley's Hardware on Saturday afternoon, Pete found himself seeing the policeman in a different light. Always before, no matter how friendly Officer Stowell seemed, in uniform or not, he remained— first and foremost—a cop. No matter how much he smiled or how friendly he seemed, he still appeared to Pete as one of those men in blue who wanted to catch Pete spray painting a wall or taking a swig out of a vodka bottle. Not a man to whom Pete could easily give his trust.

But now Bill Stowell was a man who had had the same troubles as Pete, had faced the same problems. Bill Stowell had found a solution to his problems on the football field, and he had pointed Pete in the same direction. Pete felt that Officer Stowell understood, and it made a difference.

"I didn't see your touchdown," Officer Stowell said. "I barely got there in time for the finish."

"I wondered if you were there."

The policeman gave a little chuckle and said, "Did you really almost run the wrong way?"

Pete decided he probably never would live down the one second of confusion coming out of a spin. "Well, 'almost' is not like it happened."

"I can remember having the same problem myself a couple of times."

Pete wanted to blurt out, "I know about you and the police chief years ago. I know you played for the Bulldogs—and I know why." But he said nothing, just watched the police officer's friendly face.

"You finished with a hundred and twenty-eight yards rushing. That's quite a show—for the second week in a row."

"Now I've got to make it three weeks in a row."

"You will."

Now ahead of him in the hallway, Pete saw Art and Kevin walking together toward the steps leading down to the locker room. He had to stop off at his locker to pick up his playbook, so he did not call out to them or hurry ahead to join them.

Beyond Art and Kevin, Pete saw Jimbo and Bucky approaching the outside doorway at the end of the hall.

Pete had not seen them over the weekend, had not even heard from them. He was not surprised. Jimbo would not be calling Pete after their angry words. And Bucky, as usual, was following Jimbo's lead. During the day, when Pete had been heading into a classroom with them, he had made it a point to arrive at the last minute and then to join up with someone to walk out with at the close of class.

Shoving the door open, Jimbo half turned and spotted Pete. He stopped a moment and watched Pete approaching. Bucky looked around when Jimbo stopped and gave Pete a little wave. Pete nodded back at him and continued walking toward his locker.

Pete reached his locker and turned away from Jimbo and Bucky. He twirled the dial, the lock clicked, and he opened the door.

He looked at the empty upper shelf. That was where he thought he had left his playbook. No matter—it was probably in the bottom of the locker. He placed his books on the upper shelf and then bent and rummaged through the bottom of the locker. He turned up books, a package of notebook paper, a jacket—but not the playbook.

Pete straightened up and stared into the locker. Had he left the playbook at home? He didn't remember seeing it over the weekend. No, he was sure he had left it in his locker, probably on Thursday, the day before the game. But it wasn't here. It must be at home.

He shook his head, closed the locker and twirled the dial, then turned and headed for the locker room.

◆　◆　◆　◆　◆

Dressed for practice, Pete sat down on a bench next to Tucker Williamson and stared down at the two pages—two new plays—to be inserted into the playbook.

Around him, the other players had their playbooks on their knees with the new pages laid out on top of them. Pete felt conspicuous holding the two pages in his hands and hoped that Coach Wilson would not ask about his playbook. It would be embarrassing to confess in front of everyone that he had left it at home.

Coach Wilson was speaking.

"The Hanson High defense is big and strong— but slow. We can't shove them around, but we can go around them and go through them. That's what these two plays are designed to add to our attack— to give us something that we haven't shown before, something of a surprise for them."

Pete studied the X's and O's and the squiggly lines, tracing his own assignment in each of the plays.

"Their lateral movement is slow, so we'll do a lot of running wide. This will not surprise them. The Leopards know as well as we do that they're slow moving to the outside, and they will be expecting us to try to exploit the weakness. And we will."

He paused and looked at Pete, and Pete thought for a fearful moment the coach was going to ask where his playbook was.

But Coach Wilson continued his discussion of strategy. "The two plays we added last week—getting the ball to Holman quickly out wide—will be useful against Hanson High. Also, going wide a lot of the time should set up the Hanson High defense for an occasional punch into the line."

One of the new plays was a reverse, with Tucker coming around from his wide receiver position to take the ball. It was sure to make yards against a lumbering defense. Tucker's face broke into a grin, and he said softly, "Hey, okay!"

The other play was a delayed plunge off right tackle with Art handing off to Kevin after faking a pitchout to Pete going wide to the left. The object of the delay and the fake was obvious—trick those bulky Hanson High linemen into running the wrong way.

"Study the plays tonight and we'll run them tomorrow," Coach Wilson said.

The players, some of them watching Coach Wilson, others still staring at the play pages, nodded unconsciously.

"Okay, let's get to work," Coach Wilson said.

The players got to their feet.

Pete folded the two pages in half and laid them on the shelf at the top of his locker while the other players fitted them into their ring binder playbooks.

As usual, the Monday practice was light—signal drills with no contact.

After showering and dressing, Pete scooped the play pages off the locker shelf, folded them a couple more times, and stuffed them into one of his books.

Leaving the locker room, everyone was turning left and heading for the outside door at the back of the school. Pete turned right and walked toward the steps leading up to the main floor.

"Where are you going?" Bud Perry asked.

"I've got to stop by my locker."

Pete went up the steps and walked along the empty and dimly lit hallway to his locker. He worked the combination and opened the door. The playbook had to be here! He rummaged through everything. No playbook.

He closed the locker, gave the dial a turn, and stepped back. For a moment he stood, unmoving.

He remembered that one day last week—was it Wednesday?—he had gone into Bucky's locker to clear out any of his belongings that were still in there from the first week of school.

Had he left his playbook in Bucky's locker?

No, it wasn't possible. But nevertheless he walked

the length of the hall to Bucky's locker, worked the combination, and opened the door. There was a jacket hanging on the hook, a pile of papers and books in the bottom of the locker, and a half-filled pack of cigarettes with a lighter on the shelf—but no playbook. He closed the door and spun the dial.

Almost without thinking, he walked down to Jimbo's locker and opened it. The scene inside was about the same as Bucky's—a jumble of papers and books in the bottom. But no playbook.

He must have left it at home, and then, in the excitement leading up to the Meadowcliff High game, followed by the weekend—so much happening—he had forgotten about it.

By the time Pete got home panic was beginning to take over.

He stepped through the front doorway and, as usual, began turning on lights. But this time he looked around as he flicked them on—the sofa, an overstuffed chair, his mother's desk, even the floor around the coffee table and the end tables.

No playbook.

Then he had an idea. Maybe his mother had taken it to the hospital on Saturday night or Sunday night to show to the doctors and the other nurses. He could call her at the hospital and ask. But Pete shook his head. No, that was ridiculous. His mother would never do such a thing, especially not without asking him.

He went into his room and searched—his desk, his chest of drawers, the closet shelves, the floor under the bed, even the cedar chest that held his sweaters.

No playbook.

Chapter Seventeen

In each class on Tuesday, Pete looked in the shelf under the seat of his desk on the slim chance he had left the playbook there and that it had remained unnoticed. And then, not finding it, he scanned the teacher's desk and bookshelves on the chance it had been picked up and put away, waiting to be claimed.

He decided not to ask his teachers if they had seen the playbook. The last thing he needed was his teachers mentioning in the faculty lounge—and possibly in Coach Wilson's presence—that Pete Holman had lost his playbook.

Maybe, Pete thought, a teacher had found the book and, recognizing what it was, had turned it over to Coach Wilson. If that had happened, it would solve one problem—and create another. It would be good to know that the playbook had been found and was not floating around somewhere in the wrong hands. Yes, that would be good. But bad— very bad—was the prospect of Coach Wilson's knowing that Pete had lost his playbook.

Pete remembered the coach's words when he issued him the book: "It's important that this book not fall into the wrong hands. Any player who loses his playbook is suspended for at least one game."

The recollection of the words caused Pete's face to flush. His teammates would all know what had happened: Pete Holman couldn't be trusted even to keep track of his own playbook.

Worse yet, Pete Holman's carelessness would deprive the Bulldogs of their starting running back in the game with the Hanson High Leopards. Pete Holman would have let the team down.

Probably Coach Wilson would make some sort of announcement. He would have to explain to everyone—the players, the students, the fans—why the Bulldogs' leading rusher was not even dressing out for the game. The whole world was going to know.

Even with that, there were going to be a lot of questions—from his mother, from players and students, from people around town, and from the sportswriter at the Cartwright *Morning Herald,* who would want to tell his readers what happened.

And, for sure, there would be questions from Officer Stowell. Pete dreaded that prospect most of all.

Everybody who had helped Pete and pulled for him—the coach, the policeman, the players, his mother—he had let them down, all of them.

After the bell ending the last class, Pete headed for the locker room with neither the playbook nor the slightest clue about where it was.

Pete walked into the locker room behind Alan Hollis. As usual, Alan didn't speak. Neither did Pete. Well, Alan would probably have a lot to say when everyone found out that Pete Holman had lost his playbook. Pete turned away from Alan toward the aisle where his locker was located.

"Holman!" Coach Wilson's voice, more of a bark than a call, sounded through the locker room.

Pete saw Alan turn and look at the coach in surprise. Pete turned, too.

Before Pete could answer, Coach Wilson said, "I want to talk to you. Come with me." Then, with a glance at the books under Pete's arm, he said, "Bring your books with you." The coach walked out of the locker room without looking back.

Pete glanced quickly at the gaping faces. Alan was still standing there, and Art, Kevin, and Tucker were watching. The locker room was quiet except for some voices from behind a row of lockers. Pete walked out the door behind the coach.

He followed him around a corner and into the tiny cubicle that served as the football coach's office.

By the time Pete walked through the doorway,

Coach Wilson was standing behind his desk.

A Bulldogs playbook—Pete's, for sure—was on the desk.

"Close the door."

Pete reached back and closed the door.

Coach Wilson didn't sit down, and he didn't suggest that Pete take a seat. Pete couldn't take his eyes off the playbook.

"Tell me how your playbook wound up in the hands of Coach Fulk at Hanson High."

Pete looked up at Coach Wilson. "What?"

Pete was prepared to confess that he had misplaced the playbook. He thought it was in his locker—but then it wasn't there. He was ready to admit that he did not have the slightest idea where he had left it, or even when. He was willing to accept punishment—even the suspension—with a promise that nothing like this would ever happen again.

But this—this amounted to, well, an accusation of betrayal.

"You heard me."

"I don't know," Pete said faintly.

"Somehow this playbook got from your hands into the hands of Coach Fulk at Hanson High."

"I don't know," Pete repeated, again barely above a whisper.

Coach Wilson watched him without speaking.

Then he said, "Coach Fulk drove over here personally to return the book to me this afternoon. He told me that somebody sold the book to one of his players. The player claimed he didn't know the boy who sold him the book but assumed he was a Cartwright High player." Coach Wilson paused to let that one sink in. "Coach Fulk spotted some of his players looking through the book and took it away. He said the players barely got a glance and that he didn't look at it after he recognized what it was. Luckily, Coach Fulk is an honorable man, and I believe him. But all of that is beside the point. I will ask you again. How did your playbook find its way to Hanson High?"

Pete was staring at a place low on the wall behind Coach Wilson.

The coach glared at him in silence until Pete finally looked up at him. "You have nothing to say?"

Pete looked back at the spot low on the wall and then again at Coach Wilson. "I just don't know."

"Okay. As of now, you're suspended from the team. You know the rule—lose your playbook, and you're suspended for one game. We'll get to the bottom of this, and then decide whether your suspension is permanent."

Pete walked from Coach Wilson's office to his locker in the hallway upstairs on the main floor, grateful that he didn't encounter any players asking why he was going the wrong way. At his locker, he dumped in the books he had been planning to take home. He wouldn't need them. This was not a night for homework. He slammed the locker door and wondered what Coach Wilson, at this very minute, was saying to the players in the locker room. He turned and walked out of the school.

Outside, he looked around. The area was empty except for a couple of students walking away in the distance.

Then he said one word aloud: "Jimbo."

Jimbo had the combination to his locker. Jimbo had made cracks about Pete's signing up with jocks, about thinking he was too good now for the likes of him and Bucky. Jimbo had given him that nasty grin he liked to practice on people—and a funny look as he went out the door yesterday afternoon. Jimbo had made remarks about the playbook. It had to be Jimbo.

Well, he knew where to find Jimbo Dunton in the afternoon after the last class.

Pete turned to his right and jogged the two blocks to Cartwright Avenue, the town's major traffic artery. Then, half jogging and half walking, he headed north toward the place where Cartwright Avenue went under the interstate highway and became Burton Road, leading into the neighboring suburb of Brookfield. Just beyond the interstate overpass, a road turned off, leading to the mall.

At the entrance to the mall Pete stopped, breathing heavily. He watched the people going in and out of the entrance—mothers carrying packages in one hand and clutching children with the other; men with newly purchased tools; men and women with briefcases, probably making sales calls; a couple of girls of high school age, strangers to Pete.

The best bet was the pizzeria.

Pete walked through the door and past the ground-floor displays in Windsor's department store—dresses, sweaters, shoes, handbags—and into the wide plaza, where the pizzeria was.

No Jimbo. No Bucky. No Rusty. Nobody.

He wandered around the plaza, looking in the music store, the computer store, a hamburger place, the taco stand.

Then, ahead, he spotted Bucky.

Jimbo could not be far away.

Pete broke into a fast walk through the crowd of people, trying to keep Bucky in sight. Then he saw Jimbo.

And Jimbo saw Pete.

Maybe Jimbo sensed trouble—even danger—by the mere fact that Pete was at the mall at this hour, when he should be on the practice field. Or maybe he figured that enough time had passed for everyone to know the fate of Pete's playbook. Or perhaps he just saw the expression on Pete's face. Whichever it was, Jimbo froze, both face and body. His expression went blank and stayed that way. He stood without moving.

Pete kept his eyes on Jimbo, and his mouth was almost in a smile—a frightening smile—as he worked his way through the shoppers.

Then Jimbo recovered himself. His lip curled in a small smile, and he said something to Bucky. Bucky turned and scanned the crowd. Then he saw Pete. Bucky's face went ashen. Jimbo said something else to Bucky.

Sure, Pete thought, Jimbo thought up the idea and ran the deal, and Bucky, as always, went along.

When Pete arrived in front of Jimbo, Jimbo said, "It was just a joke, Pete."

Pete heard Bucky's voice from the side. "Don't, Pete."

Jimbo was going to brazen it out, but Bucky was frightened.

Pete wanted to bash Jimbo in the face, and maybe Bucky, too, for good measure. He'd thought about it every step of the thirty-minute journey from the school. Until a few short weeks ago, he would not have bothered to give the matter any thought. He would just have done it. Alan Hollis could testify to that.

Pete clenched his fists and glared at Jimbo, now with his head tilted a little to the side, wearing the beginning of a grin, certain that Pete wasn't going to do anything in the middle of this crowd of people in the plaza.

Pete left his clenched fists at his sides.

"You're about as low as they get," he said.

Jimbo gave a little snort. "That Hanson High player didn't think so."

Pete glared at him.

He turned to Bucky, and Bucky took a quick step backward. His lips moved, but no sound came out.

"And you were in on it, too." Pete spat out the words.

"No, I—"

"You're a liar!"

"No, I didn't know he'd taken the book—until he told me to drive over to Hanson High."

"So all you did was drive him over to Hanson High with my playbook."

"Well, yeah," Bucky said uncertainly.

Pete watched the two of them a moment, then said, "You two are going with me to Coach Wilson's office in the morning and tell him what you did."

Bucky gave a little involuntary nod.

But Jimbo laughed out loud and said, "Fat chance."

Yeah, Pete thought—fat chance. Jimbo would deny everything, and he'd make sure that Bucky did the same. Where would that leave Pete?

Pete leaned his face in close to Jimbo's.

Suddenly a man in a brown uniform with a round orange patch on his shirt pocket reading Security was standing next to them. "Is there a problem here?"

Jimbo watched Pete with an air of amusement. Bucky nodded absently at the security officer.

"I don't have a problem," Pete said, "but these two jerks sure do."

Chapter Eighteen

When Pete got home, the house was empty and darkening with the shadows of the late afternoon. It was Tuesday, normally his mother's day off from the hospital, but she was working another swap with Elaine so she could watch Pete play against Hanson High on Friday night. Pete gave a little snort at the irony and turned on the lights in the living room.

He dropped onto the sofa, still breathing heavily from the long trip from the mall, most of it jogging.

As he leaned back he gave a little nod and tried to tell himself that everything was going to be all right, now that he knew what had really happened. It was just a matter of time—time for explanation, time for questions and answers. Then everything was going to be straightened out. He told himself that he was sure of it.

The pictures of Jimbo's sneer and Bucky's fright were gone from his mind almost as soon as he had walked away. Leaving them standing with the security guard in the plaza, he'd felt a great satisfaction—

even a sense of triumph—in the fact that he had not hit Jimbo in the face. In the past, that had been Pete Holman's solution to any dispute—a fist in the face. Oh, he had wanted to hit Jimbo. But he hadn't done it.

On the way home, moving along the sidewalks, crossing the streets, Pete had turned his mind to his next move. For sure, Jimbo wasn't going to offer any confessions to help Pete out of the jam. At his best, Jimbo was not much of one for doing favors. And in this case he would be incriminating himself. No, Jimbo wasn't going to do it. That was for certain. Worse yet, nobody was going to be able to force Jimbo to tell the truth. Jimbo was as good at lying as, well, Pete Holman used to be. And Jimbo would be able to keep Bucky in line.

So Pete would have to tell Coach Wilson what had happened—and would have to convince the coach that he was telling the truth. Maybe Coach Wilson would accept Pete's account. Maybe he would insist on questioning Jimbo. Probably he would. Yes, Jimbo would lie, but Coach Wilson would see through it. He had to. Then, in the end, the coach would believe Pete. He had to. Everything was going to be all right. It had to be.

Everything, that is, except one thing. A nagging thought returned to his mind now as he sat forward on the sofa, elbows on his knees. However it had happened, the fact remained that Pete had indeed lost his playbook, and the price for that was a one-game suspension.

Well, he thought, maybe theft was an exception.

Pete glanced at the clock on his mother's desk—quarter to six.

The players had long since finished their practice. They'd run their wind sprints, had their showers, and dressed, and about now they were on their way home. They knew that something was wrong with Pete. He'd missed practice. But what else did they know? Pete wondered what Coach Wilson had told them. If the coach had told them that Pete Holman's playbook had wound up in the hands of a Hanson High player, what were his teammates saying about him? Pete didn't have any trouble guessing, and he frowned.

Coach Wilson also would be heading home, and Pete considered calling him. He could tell the coach what he'd learned, maybe get the whole problem resolved right away, then sleep well tonight and move ahead tomorrow as if nothing had happened. It sounded like a good scenario with a happy ending.

But Pete shook his head silently. No, he had to speak to Coach Wilson face-to-face. He had to convince him he was telling the truth. And he had to convince him that the loss of the playbook wasn't his fault. He wanted to see the coach's face while he talked. And he wanted Coach Wilson to see *his* face. He would seek out the coach at the end of the lunch period the next day—no later.

The telephone rang, startling Pete.

Then he listened to it ring a second time. The caller certainly wasn't one of his old friends—Jimbo, Bucky, Rusty. And the caller surely wasn't one of his new friends—Art, Bud, Kevin—not if they believed that Pete had allowed his playbook to fall into the hands of a Hanson High player.

With a feeling of dread, he considered the possibility that the caller was Officer Stowell.

He got up, walked across to the desk, and picked up the telephone. "Hello."

"What happened?"

He frowned and didn't answer. He didn't recognize the voice.

"This is Art."

Pete didn't speak for a moment. He wished he had left the ringing telephone unanswered. Then he said, "Oh, hi."

"What happened?" Art repeated.

Instead of answering the question, Pete asked, "What did Coach Wilson say?"

"Nothing. Just that you wouldn't be at practice.

That was all—nothing else. We were all wondering what was wrong."

Pete took a couple of breaths. Was Art just being nosy? No, he had been friendly from the start, and he sounded genuinely concerned now. "Do you have time to listen to a long story?"

"Yeah, sure."

Pete sat down, his elbows on the desk, the telephone pressed to his ear, and started talking. He began with being unable to find his playbook in his locker. He told of his frantic searches, the increasing panic. Then he related Coach Wilson's stern words in his office and the horrible sight of the missing playbook on his desk. He ended with the angry confrontation with Jimbo and Bucky in the plaza of the mall.

The line was silent for a moment. Then Art said, "That's the dirtiest trick I ever heard of."

"Yeah, me too—but there it is."

"Have you told Coach Wilson?"

"Not yet. I'll see him tomorrow." Then he added, "I hope he'll believe me."

"He will. Don't worry."

When Pete arrived at school the next morning, one of the first familiar faces he encountered in the lobby was Bud Perry's. "We're all behind you," Bud said. "It's going to be okay."

Pete looked at Bud, at first surprised that he knew what had happened. Then he mumbled a word of thanks.

The expressions of support continued through the morning as Pete met various players in his classroom and in the hallways, and he concluded that Art must have had a busy evening on the telephone. Well, that was okay. It saved him from having to answer questions at every turn.

At midmorning he walked out of a class with Art. "Have you spoken with Coach Wilson yet?" Art asked.

"Not yet."

"When are you going to do it?"

Pete glanced at Art. "At the end of the lunch period. We'll both have a few free minutes out of class, and there probably won't be anyone around his office."

Pete saw Jimbo twice and Bucky once during the morning. Pete glared and said nothing. Jimbo gave Pete a smirk the first time they met, but on the second encounter he was wearing a sort of questioning expression. Maybe Jimbo was wondering if Pete had reported what he'd learned to the coach— and if the coach was going to be calling him in for some answers.

At noon, Pete went through the lunch line with Bryan. He saw Jimbo and Bucky ahead of them and watched the two carry their trays to the usual table. Pete then walked with Bryan to a table where several football players were seated.

As he sat down, he looked over his shoulder in the direction of the long faculty table in the corner. Coach Wilson was there.

He glanced across at Jimbo and Bucky, now joined by Rusty. They were talking and not looking at him.

When Pete finished his lunch, he got to his feet, glanced at Art across from him, gave a little shrug, and said, "Well, here goes."

"Right," Art said.

As he turned and began walking across the cafeteria toward the faculty table, all the football players at the table got to their feet.

Pete heard the half dozen or so chairs scraping the floor and looked back at the players standing in their places. Art was smiling. Bud waved.

Coach Wilson spotted Pete approaching and got to his feet, unsmiling. Other teachers at the table were turning and looking at Pete. It was unusual for a student to walk across to the faculty table during the lunch period. But more than that, Pete wondered if the coach had told the teachers the story of his playbook.

As Pete walked around to Coach Wilson's side of the table, he saw out of the corner of his eye his teammates—Art, Bud, Tucker, Bryan, Kevin, Leon, and, to his surprise, Alan—moving as a group across the cafeteria toward the table where Jimbo and his friends were seated.

Pete took a breath and spoke to the coach. "Coach Wilson, could I see you in your office? I've found out—"

Before Pete could finish his sentence, Coach Wilson nodded and said, "All right."

Beyond the coach, Pete saw Jimbo, a look of alarm on his face, get to his feet as the football players encircled him. What was happening?

Coach Wilson, with his back to Jimbo's table as he spoke to Pete, walked toward the door, unaware of what was happening, and Pete followed with one puzzled look back.

Walking behind the coach out of the cafeteria, down a hallway, around two corners, and into his office, Pete tried to frame what he was going to say. It had all seemed so easy last night when he'd rehearsed the story he was going to tell. But now it didn't seem easy at all.

Coach Wilson entered his office, walked around behind his desk, and said nothing for a moment. He just looked at Pete. Then he gestured at the chair, said, "Sit down," and seated himself. Pete glanced at the open door before he sat down, but he made no move to close it.

His playbook, marked with the number 22, remained on Coach Wilson's desk.

The coach said, "Well?"

Pete took a deep breath and said, "Jimbo Dunton stole my playbook from my locker and took it to Hanson High." He stopped. There it was—the whole story in one sentence. Now what?

Coach Wilson watched Pete without speaking. Did he believe Pete? Or did he think that the old Pete Holman—the troublemaker—was trying to frame a classmate to escape blame?

Pete waited with the coach in the silence. He could feel his heart beating.

Then Coach Wilson spoke. "What does Jimbo Dunton have to say about this?"

Before Pete could answer, Art spoke from the doorway. "Jimbo is going to tell you that it's true."

Chapter Nineteen

Pete turned in his chair with a start and got to his feet. There was Art, standing in the doorway. And next to him, looking shaken, was Jimbo. Behind them, Pete saw the other faces—Bud, Kevin, Leon, and, off to the side, Tucker, Bryan, and Alan.

"Jimbo wants to tell you about it."

Coach Wilson was on his feet now.

Pete looked at Art, then at Jimbo, and then turned and looked at Coach Wilson. Pete shook his head slightly as if to say he didn't know what was happening.

Coach Wilson stared at the scene in the doorway and said nothing.

"Go on, Jimbo," Art said.

Jimbo wasn't looking at anyone. He was looking at the floor. When he spoke, the words came out as a mixture of a mumble and a whisper. "It's true," he said. "Pete's right. I got his playbook out of his locker. I was just joking. I didn't mean to make any

166

trouble." He gave Pete a quick glance, then looked at Art.

"There's more," Art said.

Jimbo took a breath, returned his gaze to the floor, and said, "I took the book to Hanson High and sold it to a boy." After another breath, he looked up at Coach Wilson and added, "I didn't think it was going to hurt anything."

Pete stared at Jimbo, and a scary thought raced through his mind. A month ago, this might have been Pete Holman standing there confessing that he had stolen a playbook and sold it to an opposing player.

The bell rang, ending the lunch period.

Coach Wilson finally spoke. "Art, you and the others go on to your classes. Pete, wait here with me for a minute."

When Jimbo turned with the players to leave, Coach Wilson snapped, "Dunton, you stay." Jimbo stopped and stood in the doorway.

Pete turned to Coach Wilson.

"I'm glad it ended this way," the coach said. "I never believed that you had sold the book to that Hanson High player. But it did look like you had lost it through carelessness and that the wrong person had found it. I'm happy that wasn't the case."

Pete nodded.

Coach Wilson sat down and picked up a pencil and notepad. "I'll write you a tardiness excuse in case you're late arriving for class." He scrawled something on the paper and handed it to Pete.

"I'll need one, too," Jimbo said.

"No, you won't. I'll be escorting you to the principal's office, and he can decide when you'll be going back to a classroom."

Pete started toward the door.

"Holman!"

Pete stopped and turned.

"You're forgetting your playbook." Coach Wilson picked up the ring binder and handed it to Pete. "You want to be careful that you don't leave it somewhere."

Pete grinned and took the book.

When the last class ended, Pete stepped into the hallway and looked to his left, where he knew Art would be leaving a classroom.

The assistant principal, Mr. Owen, walked by. Pete hadn't seen him since he and Bucky were assigned to early morning study hall. That had been a grim scene. But this time the assistant principal smiled at Pete, gave a little nod, and said, "Good luck on Friday night, Pete."

"Thanks," Pete said, returning the smile.

Spotting Art coming out of his class, Pete called

to him and hurried down the hallway to join him for the walk to the locker room.

"How did you get Jimbo to confess?"

"Well," Art said with a grin, "there were seven of us, and we just kind of talked him into it."

"I've never been so surprised in my life."

"We talked about it this morning before the first class and decided you needed some backup for your story—backup from Jimbo. So we told Jimbo that we knew the truth, and that we thought it would be nice if he came with us to Coach Wilson's office. He acted brave at first, but then he agreed."

Pete watched Art.

Art grinned at him again. "Nobody hit him, if that's what you're wondering."

"Uh-huh."

"But," Art continued, "I'll admit that Jimbo did have reason to worry."

Pete turned toward Art as they walked along. "Look, I really appreciate you—all of you guys—you—" He struggled to find the right words. Pete Holman did not have a lot of experience expressing gratitude. "What I mean is—"

Art gave a little dismissive wave of his hand. "Please don't make a speech. We get enough speeches from Coach Wilson during the season."

They were at the top of the stairs leading down to the locker room. Pete stopped, and Art stopped with him. "Okay, no speech. But I want to ask you something."

"What?"

Pete stepped to the side of the corridor and Art followed him. "You've been okay to me from the very start. I mean, you helped me and you were friendly." Pete paused, and his remark to Officer Stowell flashed through his mind—nobody does anything for nothing. That had been Pete Holman's credo. But now it seemed that a lot of people were doing things for nothing. He'd found out about Officer Stowell's motives. But what about Art? He decided not to repeat the remark to Art. Instead, he said, "And this stuff with Jimbo…"

Art watched Pete a moment, a serious expression on his face. Then he said, "There's no mystery to it. The first moment you stepped on the practice field, you were a member of the Bulldogs. I wanted you to do well, same as you wanted me to do well. That's what a team is all about. We help one another."

"I see. I think I really do see."

They went down the stairs.

Officer Stowell was standing alongside the door to the locker room. Art gave him a small nod of greeting and went inside. Pete stopped, and the policeman stepped forward.

"I was on patrol duty last night and didn't hear anything about this problem until today, when Coach Wilson called me. I told him I was sure there was some misunderstanding. I'm glad it's all cleared up now."

"I wondered if you knew."

"It must have been a tough time for you. You should've called me."

Pete smiled at the policeman. "Yeah, I think so now myself. But at the time I was wondering if anyone would ever believe me again. Anyway, it's over."

The officer watched Pete. "It's good to have teammates, isn't it?"

"You bet, and I've got to talk to one of them right now, before practice starts."

"See you on the practice field."

"Right—and thanks. Thanks for everything."

Pete walked through the doorway into the locker room and almost bumped into Alan Hollis.

"I was waiting for you," Alan said.

"And I was looking for you."

"What?"

"I want to thank you for being there today, and to give you a long-overdue apology. Last spring— outside English Lit class—I was wrong."

"Okay. I was there today because nobody deserves the dirty deal Jimbo Dunton was giving you." Alan grinned and added, "Not even Pete Holman." He paused. "And I was wrong to make a joke about you in English Lit."

Pete stuck out his hand, and Alan took it. "So, okay, we're even."

Coach Wilson walked by. "Are you two going to get dressed or just stand there congratulating each other?"